the Wrong Train

Jeremy de Quidt

illustrated by Dave Shelton

David Fickling Books
31 Beaumont Street
Oxford OX1 2NP, UK

The Wrong Train
is a
DAVID FICKLING BOOK

First published in Great Britain by
David Fickling Books,
31 Beaumont Street,
Oxford, OX1 2NP

www.davidficklingbooks.com

Hardback edition published 2016
This edition published 2017

Text © Jeremy de Quidt
Illustrations © Dave Shelton

978-1-910989-50-0

1 3 5 7 9 10 8 6 4 2

Papers used by David Fickling Books are from well-managed forests
and other responsible sources.

MIX
Paper from
responsible sources
FSC
www.fsc.org   FSC® C016897

DAVID FICKLING BOOKS Reg. No. 8340307

A CIP catalogue record for this book is available from the British Library.

Typeset in 11.5/15.5 pt Sabon by Falcon Oast Graphic Art Ltd.
Printed and bound in Great Britain by Clays Ltd, St Ives plc.

the Wrong Train

www.davidficklingbooks.com

Also by Jeremy de Quidt

The Toymaker
The Feathered Man

For Lizzie, Jack, Alice and Bea,
same lovely sailors,
same leaky sieve.

The boy didn't realise what he'd done at first because the train was where the last train should have been – a little two-carriage diesel at the end of the platform – and he'd run flat out to catch it.

Putting his feet up on the seat opposite and getting his breath back, he sat looking down the carriage at the long black line of windows and the strip lights reflected in the glass, and even then the penny didn't drop. There were usually at least half a dozen other people on the last train, but the carriage was empty. It was just him.

There was enough charge left on his phone to ring his dad to tell him he'd caught the train, so his dad could pick him up, and then the phone died. But that didn't matter because his dad would be at the station, and it was only three stops.

It dawned on him only slowly that there was

something wrong – *a thought that there should have been a station by now began to rise up through his head, like a child tugging at his sleeve for attention, and he sat up in the seat. Cupping his hands to the window and blanking out the lights of the carriage, all he could see was dark, and that was what was wrong. Breath condensing against the cold glass he rubbed it clear and looked again, but there was nothing to see. Only dark.*

What started as suspicion became certainty as the train rolled on and no familiar lights drifted past the window – not the flyover across the road, or the floodlights of the petrol station.

This wasn't the right train.

He stuck his face to the glass and stared out, trying to work out where he was, but there were no clues, not one – no station, no sign, nothing. He desperately wanted the train to stop so he could get off, but it just kept on going. Fifteen minutes – twenty? He sat looking helplessly at the empty carriage and the dark mirrors of the windows while the sound of the diesel droned on, taking him he hadn't a clue where.

At last, the train began to slow. For several minutes it crawled along as though on the point of stopping, but never actually did, and each time he thought it would, it began to pick up speed again.

Finally the train juddered to a halt in the dark, and he didn't even know whether it was at a station or not, because cupping his hands to the glass there were only a few lights and a low concrete wall to be seen out of the window. But the light on the door button came on, and being off the train seemed a better deal than being on it. So, getting out of his seat, he stepped onto the cold, dark platform before he'd even really thought through whether that was a good idea or not.

Hearing the doors of the train close behind him, and the engine revving up and pulling away leaving him there in the dark and the cold, he wasn't so sure it had been a good idea at all. There was no one else on the platform, but by then it was too late to do anything except watch the lights of the train disappear. When the sound of it couldn't be heard any more, there was no sound at all.

Just silence.

It didn't even look like a real station. The slab concrete of the wall ran along the back of it and there was a little shelter with a bench, but nothing else – not a ticket office or a machine. Not even a sign to say where it was. He could see the ends of the platform sloping down to the tracks and there were three lamps on poles, but the light from them was thin and weak. There were no houses, no street

3

lights. So far as he could see, there wasn't a road, not even steps down to one. It was just a platform, dark and still, in the middle of nowhere.

Pulling his coat round him he tried laughing at the dumbness of what he'd done, but in the cold silence his laughter fell from his lips like a shot bird, and that made him feel more alone. Sitting down on the bench, he turned up his collar against the cold and wondered what on earth he was going to do.

He'd been sitting like that for a while before he noticed the light.

At first it was so small that he wasn't sure what it was – just a tiny dot swinging to and fro. But as it came slowly nearer, grew larger, he realised it was a torch.

No, not a torch.

A lantern.

A glass lantern.

Someone carrying a lantern was walking along the railway tracks, out of the darkness, towards him.

He sat up, not quite sure what to make of this. But as the light came closer, came slowly up the slope of the platform's end, any concerns he might have had evaporated as he saw that it was carried by an old man. The man held the lantern in one hand, and a shopping bag and a lead attached to a small dog in the other. He came unhurriedly along the platform and, stopping by the bench, looked down at the boy and then up and back along the platform in that vague, undecided way that small children and elderly people do. The little dog sniffed at the boy's shoes.

The boy sat looking at the man – at the frayed collar and thumb-greased tie, the thin raincoat, the cheap, split plastic leatherette of the shopping bag, the worn shoes and the scruffy little grey dog. A bunch of dead leaves and withered flowers poked out of the top of the bag and that didn't seem quite right.

The boy grinned apologetically.

'I'm sorry,' he said. 'But could you tell me when the next train's going to be? I got on the wrong one and I need to get on one going back the other way.'

The old man glanced down at him, but didn't say anything and the boy wasn't sure whether he'd heard or not, so he said it again, and this time the man turned his head and looked at him.

'It's not a station,' he said brightly. 'It's a Permanent Way Post. You're on a Permanent Way Post.'

He had an odd voice – sing-song, and brittle like a reed. Without seeing the face it could have been a man's or a woman's.

'I'm sorry, I don't understand,' said the boy.

5

The man looked back along the track and, lifting the hand that held the lead and the bag, he pointed at the rails.

'It's what the railway workers use when they mend the tracks,' he said. 'It's not a station.'

'But the train stopped here,' the boy objected. 'I got off it.'

'Well, you shouldn't have done that,' the man laughed. 'You shouldn't have done that at all. I wouldn't have come along if you hadn't done that.'

The boy didn't understand what the man meant by that either, but the man sat himself down on the bench next to him and smiled reassuringly, so he smiled back. Up close, the man's clothes smelled of washing powder and old cloth – it was a homely smell, like cups of tea and newsagents. The man put the lantern on the ground between his feet. It lit his socks and his shoes, the grubby grey coat of the little dog. The boy could see his eyes now, they were watering in the cold night air. The man smiled again.

'If you're stuck here,' he said. 'Toby and me better keep you company. Least, until your train comes. We've got plenty of time, me and Toby.'

The little dog looked up and wagged its tail.

The boy pulled his coat tighter, pressed out the cold pockets of air and folded his arms round him to keep the warmth in.

'It's all right,' he said. 'Really, I'm fine – as long as I know there's another train going to come.'

But as he said it, he looked along the empty platform and, if he was honest with himself, he thought he'd be glad of the company.

'Wouldn't dream of leaving you,' said the old man. 'Not now you've got off the train. Wouldn't be right for me to leave you, would it?' He smiled and, bending forward, stroked the little dog's ears.

The boy frowned. 'It will stop, won't it?' he asked, looking along the bare platform.

'Course it will,' the man said. 'Just wave it down, and you'll be all right.'

They sat quietly for a while. The man didn't say anything, he sat looking into the dark at the end of the platform, tapping his shoes on the cold ground, one then the other, as though drumming a little tune to himself while he watched for the lights of the train. The boy began to think that things hadn't worked out so badly. All he had to do was wait for the train. If he'd only been able to ring his dad, he wouldn't have minded at all.

He breathed out, making clouds with his breath, trying to pile one breath on top of the other.

The novelty of doing that was just beginning to wear thin, when the man turned and looked at him.

'I'll tell you what we'll do,' he said. 'I'll tell you a

story while we wait for your train – help pass the time, a nice little story will. It's a long time since I've told anyone one of my stories.'

'You don't have to,' the boy said. 'Really, I'm all right.'

But the man smiled, only this time it seemed he was smiling more to himself than to the boy.

'Got a little brother, have you?' he asked.

There was something so penetrating about the eyes that looked out of that old face, that the boy didn't need to answer.

'I thought so,' the man said. 'I know a story about a girl and her baby brother. I'll tell you that one if you like – help pass the time, it will.'

The boy shook his head resignedly.

'All right, then,' he said.

'Tickety-boo,' said the old man brightly, and sitting back on the bench, he took a quiet breath, and began.

It happened so seamlessly as the man spoke that the boy couldn't say when the platform stopped and the small house started, but once it had happened there wasn't a platform around him any more – there was only the sense of a summer sky, and green leaves, and a girl standing on a dirt track that led to a small house.

Nanny's Little Candle

It was her mum's idea to move. 'New baby, new house,' she'd said.

But the baby wasn't Cassie's dad's, and Cassie didn't have a dad any more, not since he'd found that out. So now it was just Cassie, and her mum and the new baby.

'It will be lovely,' her mum kept saying. 'Everything you didn't have in the town, everything you've always wanted – big garden, trees to climb. You can walk down the track and get the bus to the new school when you start in the autumn. It'll be simple.'

But she was thirteen now. She'd wanted the tree and the garden when she was eight, but not now. It was like her mum couldn't see that. It wasn't even going to be her old school. Everything had to be new – Mum's new smile, Mum's new plans, Mum's new baby – everything.

Everything, that is, except for the bungalow at the end of the track. There was nothing new about that. It was from the 1930s – bit of a garden, bit of an orchard – all overgrown. When the old lady who'd lived there died it just stood empty. Wasn't even cleared of her things. After a year, it was put up for rent – a big red sign at the end of the track – that's how Cassie's mum found it.

It was falling down, but it was cheap. When they moved in the old lady's furniture was still there – not the beds and sheets, they'd all gone – but everything else; chairs, table, cracked bar of soap on the window sill, old pages out of a *Women's Weekly* sellotaped to the wall. Her TV licence pinned to one side of the kitchen mirror. There was even a calendar with her hospital appointments marked on it in pen.

It smelled damp. Felt damp.

'It won't do, not once we've got the place all cleaned and aired,' her mum had said. She'd gone round singing a happy cleaning song like she was some princess in a film, opening the windows – the panes all dirty with old rain and dust. 'Listen, Cassie,' she'd said as she'd stood by a window, and Cassie had listened. There was nothing, just birds singing and insects in the orchard. No street, no cars, no noise. Nothing of their old life at all.

'You see, love?' her mum had said, smiling. 'You see?'

There was a cubby-hole kitchen with a couple of painted shelves and a two-ring gas hob, lino tiles on the floor. A rusty little key that didn't fit anything hung knotted on a string in the larder like it had been there for ever.

Cassie's room was at the back. From the window she could see the orchard thick with summer nettles and weeds. There were thirteen apple trees and beyond them, at the edge of the open fields, a water butt and an old brick-and-plaster outbuilding with the roof all fallen in.

There was so much work, so much cleaning to do. The water and the electricity didn't always work though, and when they didn't her mum would ring the renting agents on her mobile, only there was barely enough signal to make herself heard and she'd just end up shouting at them.

Sometimes, after Cassie had gone to bed, she'd hear her mum ringing 'Michael', whoever he was, and she'd end up shouting at him too.

And then there was the baby.

All those times her mum had told her and Dad that she'd been working late, well, it hadn't always been work, had it?

Her mum had called the baby 'Niall', which sounded like the river. Cassie just called it 'the baby'.

'His name's Niall,' her mum would say. She wouldn't give up trying to get Cassie to say his name, but it wasn't something Cassie wanted to do. If it hadn't been for it, things wouldn't have changed, would they? She'd have been back in the old house with her mum and her dad and it would have been just the three of them like it always had.

But it wasn't.

She didn't even want to hold the baby. Just

thinking about her mum holding it made her feel physically sick.

'Go on, you have a go,' her mum would say, but Cassie wouldn't take him. Her mum would rub her own face against the baby's soft, downy black hair and say, 'He smells like biscuits and vanilla. Go on, you'll like it when you do.' But Cassie didn't want to, and finally her mum would turn away and stand by the open back door holding the baby and looking out at the thick nettles and the weeds in the orchard, and Cassie almost didn't care if she was crying or not, because the baby cried enough for both of them.

He hardly ever stopped – least that's what Cassie thought.

Not that what she thought seemed to matter to anyone any more. She couldn't even talk to her old friends about any of it because the mobile signal was so crap.

So she made do the best she could; lying on her bed listening to her music, to Niall crying, to her mum trying to pretend that everything was princess-land wonderful.

And then, Cassie found the little wooden box.

It was in the old outbuilding. She'd got to it across the orchard, cutting her way through the tall nettles with a stick. The plaster on the walls was rust stained and blooming with yellow mould, and there was a big metal pot filled with a mush of wet leaves that stank when she stirred them. The ground was covered with broken roof tiles and twigs and pigeon droppings, but in one corner was a wooden box – not much bigger than a shoe box. The wood was warped and weather-stained and there was a little brass key plate on the front. It was locked tight. But the box rattled when she shook it, so there had to be something inside. She took it back through the nettles.

'There won't be anything worth having,' her mum said as Cassie tried the kitchen drawers for a screwdriver to prise it open. 'It's probably just old tools.'

But Cassie didn't care.

Only, she couldn't find a screwdriver.

As if someone had whispered the idea into her head, she suddenly remembered the rusty little key on the string in the larder.

That would be about the right size. She pulled it off its string and tried it in the lock.

Bingo.

With a little bit of careful effort, it turned.

She couldn't believe her disappointment. There were four old candles in the box, that was all. They were wrapped in yellowed wax paper – three white ones and a black one. The black one was dirty and greasy. Cassie had to wipe her fingers clean on her top after she'd touched it.

'I said it wouldn't be anything worthwhile,' said her mum, standing there, Niall on her hip.

'I think they're good,' said Cassie, but she didn't know why she'd said that because they weren't good at all. She could still feel the greasiness of the black candle on the tips of her fingers. But when her mum said to put them back outside where she'd found them, Cassie didn't want to. They were hers now. She put them on the old lady's dressing table that was in her room.

They were still there when she went to bed.

It wasn't that she'd meant to light them, and if she'd had any batteries left in her torch when she went to bed, she wouldn't have done. But when the electricity went off that night after tea they were the only candles they had. Rather than go to bed in the dark, Cassie stood the four candles in a plate of water on the dresser and lit them with a match. First the white ones and then, the last of the match almost burning her fingers, she lit the black.

She lay in her bed watching as the flickering shadows crept upwards and forwards across the wall. Her mum had gone to bed. Through the thin walls she could hear the sound of Niall crying and her mum shushing and singing little songs to him, like she used to do to Cassie when she cried.

Only, her mum didn't do that for her any more.

Cassie punched her pillow flat and with the candles still burning and the shadows reaching out across the walls, she put her headphones in, turned her music up to drown out the sound of the baby, and closed her eyes.

She let the words and the music wash over her. The sheets were cool and her body felt long and still. She lay there, all quiet with the music in her head. But there was a whispering line in one of the songs she'd never noticed before. Someone was speaking along to the music, only it didn't fit the song. It was reedy, like an old woman's voice.

'. . . Hangman's noose snuffed out my light, burn little candle nice and bright . . .'

Over and over again.

She heard it in the next song too, and finally, as slowly as though coming to her through syrup, she realised that wasn't how any of the songs went, and that she was dreaming.

She opened her eyes, but even as she did, she knew that the dream was still going on because the room that she saw wasn't her room. It was a cold, bare kitchen and where the dresser should have been there was an iron cooking range with a shelf above it. A dirty rag-rug lay on a stone floor. There was a chair, a table with a couple of house bricks on it – red and brown. She knew the room was quite dark because it was night time, but in the way of dreams she didn't question for one moment that she was able to see everything that was there quite clearly, right down to the colour of the bricks. On the shelf above the range, was a black candle – its flame burning with a dirty, greasy smoke, as though the candle had been made from fat and skin, not wax. Its flame drifted lazily in a draught, but it cast no light, no shadows. If anything it made the room even darker still.

She lay staring at the kitchen and candle.

As she watched, the door latch lifted and an elderly woman came in. She was dressed as no one dressed any more – in a long thick skirt with a black bonnet and a shawl, and she was carrying a leather bag. She put it down on the table. There was something inside the bag, but Cassie couldn't see what it was. She could hear Niall crying now – she even had to listen to him in her dreams. It was almost as if the old woman could hear him too, because she glanced irritably down at the bag as though the sound of his crying was coming from there. But the woman didn't do anything about it. She tipped her purse out and began counting onto the table a whole handful of coins, then she scooped them up and, crossing the room, dropped them into a jar on the shelf beside the candle. The flame guttered darkly.

Only then did the woman turn and look at the

bag. There was a different expression on her face now – wicked and deliberate. She lifted her eyes and looked straight at Cassie. Cassie could only watch dumbly as the woman took a cloth down from the shelf and began folding it into a small pad. When she'd done, she walked back to the table and opened the bag. The sound of crying was suddenly louder and Cassie realised that it was coming from inside the bag, not from Niall. With one hand the woman held the bag open and with the other she reached in with the pad of cloth and, pressing it down, stood there like that for as long as it took for all the crying to stop.

When there was no more noise, she looked up from the bag and smiled at Cassie. It was a cruel smile. Picking up the bricks she dropped them into the bag and snapped the clasp shut.

Then, Cassie wasn't looking at the kitchen any more. She was standing on the bank of a river by a deep pool and it was dark and cold, and she was watching a leather bag sink slowly out of sight.

With a start, she opened her eyes wide. The ripples in the dark pool, the river bank, they'd all gone.

There was sunlight on the pillow by her cheek. She sat bolt upright and looked at the room, her breath stuffed up in her chest. There was nothing, no range, no rug, no table. For a moment, she could have said exactly where they'd stood, but even as she looked the image faded and disappeared. It was just her room with sunlight streaming in. But she was shaking.

On the dresser the candles had melted and run over the plate into one dirty mess. The room smelled of burning and stale fat. She got out of bed, the lino damp and cold on her feet. She opened the window, retching and breathing in great lungfuls of fresh air.

She felt sick.

It must have been the candles, she thought. They'd done carbon monoxide at school – maybe it was like that? She could have suffocated and no one would have known. It had been like a poison.

She stood there breathing in the clean cool air. She could hear her mum moving about in the kitchen, the radio on, the sound of the baby crying.

Like the crying from the bag.

Her tongue felt fat and dirty in her mouth. Her head ached. She sat on the edge of her bed and tried not to remember the dream.

But she couldn't forget the dream.

She still didn't feel well when it was time for her mum to go into town to get the shopping – it was the big shop too. But her mum didn't believe her when she said she felt too sick to go – she'd done that before to get out of the shop – only this time she really did feel sick, and her mum didn't believe her. She tried to tell her that it was the smell of the candles, tried to tell her about the dream, about the baby in the bag. But when she told her about that – about the baby in the leather bag – her mum's face had gone white-pale like it only did when she was really angry, and there was nothing Cassie could say or do to put it right then. It ended with her mum calling her vicious and selfish and spoilt – and a whole lot else besides that was to do with her dad, not her – and then her mum put Niall and the buggy and all the rest of his stuff into the car and drove off without Cassie.

That's how it always ended up these days – Cassie on her own and her mum with the baby. It never used to be like that.

It was never like that.

Her mum hit the brakes hard at the end of the track, she drove like that when she was really angry. The car swung out onto the road and the noise of it grew fainter until there was nothing left but the quiet, and a taste in Cassie's mouth like dirty wax.

For a while she sat on the wooden back steps with her headphones in just looking out at the orchard and wishing that she'd gone with her mum. Wishing that her mum would come back so she could say sorry to her.

But her mum didn't come back.

As time wore on Cassie began to feel more and more uncomfortable sitting there. It was an unpleasant sensation, and it grew stronger by the moment. She knew she was alone, only it didn't feel like it. She took one headphone out and looked round at the orchard, at the long track to the road – but there was no one there.

Quite clearly, from inside the bungalow behind her, she heard a sound.

A baby crying.

Just for a moment she thought that it must be Niall and her mum had come back, only there hadn't been a car, so it couldn't have been.

'Mum?'

There was no answer, just the sound of a baby crying. Only it wasn't like the racket that Niall made – it was faint and sickly, like the mewing of a kitten.

She got unsteadily to her feet. Holding onto the door frame she stepped into the kitchen, and pulling out the other headphone she cocked her head and listened again. The sound was coming from along the passage.

Coming from her bedroom.

More puzzled than afraid, because it sounded like a cat, she went down the little narrow passage and, pausing by the door to listen, turned the handle and opened it.

She was looking again at the flagstoned kitchen with the iron range, only now it was daylight. The woman was there – shawl and skirt and buttoned boots. She didn't seem to notice Cassie. She was pouring hot milk from a pan into a stoneware baby's bottle – Cassie could see the baby in a basket on the floor at her feet – but the milk was far too hot. Cassie could see the steam rising from the pan – you can't give a baby scalding milk.

The woman turned, looked straight at her, and smiled – and then Cassie didn't know whether it was real or not because the iron range and the bottle, the woman and the baby, they weren't there. It was just her room and her bed and the sunlight. It happened so quickly – like when you think you've seen a bird and you look again and it's just an old brown leaf, and you don't know whether you even saw a bird at all.

That's how it was.

The woman was there

then gone.

Cassie stood in the open doorway looking at the empty room, at the turned-back duvet, her clothes on the floor. Her head was aching and she didn't feel well. She wanted to cry now – didn't want to wait on her own for her mum.

Not there.

She took her back door key down from the peg on the fridge, locked the door and went out onto the track, down towards the road. There was a shop in the village. Nearer than the shop was the church. There was a bench just inside the gate. She could sit there in the sun and watch for her mum.

A man was cutting the grass. She sat on the bench listening to the sound of the mower and watching the road, but it didn't make her feel any better. She must have dozed, because the church clock woke her.

The sun had moved round. When she opened her eyes the first thing she saw amongst the headstones was a small white marble statue of a little girl holding a dove. She hadn't noticed it before, but now the sun was actually shining on it. She stretched and stood up. Walked over and read the lead-lettered inscription:

IN MEMORY OF THE INFANTS OF THE WEIR POND. JUNE 1888.

There was a weir in the river on the other side of the church, she'd seen it from a distance – a pool with willows on the banks.

And suddenly she knew the place—
a dark pool with willows on the banks,
and a leather bag sinking out of sight.
Something cold had touched her.

She looked again at the date and the style of clothes the little girl wore – at the buttoned boots and the shawl.

She could taste dirty black wax in her mouth.

There weren't any names on the marble, it just said 'infants'.

She looked about her. The man who'd been mowing the grass had finished. He'd put the mower away and was coming up the path towards the gate – an old man, flat cap in his hand. The village was full of them. She tried to stop him.

'Excuse me?' she said loudly.

He smelled of sweat and tobacco and tweed coat, and he passed her by.

'What's this about?' she said, pointing at the marble statue. 'This one.'

But he kept walking, and then she felt stupid and angry just to be left standing there like that.

Beyond the churchyard wall she saw the roof of her mum's car go past. It turned up the track.

Her mum had a way of talking when they'd had a row – short, like a series of statements, not waiting for a reply – and she wouldn't stop what she was doing either. Wouldn't look at Cassie. She was already unpacking the shopping when Cassie got back to the bungalow, and that's what it was like then.

'I gave a lift to an old woman,' her mum said, pulling things out of the bags on the table and putting them on the shelves. 'She was just walking along the road back from town. Had a big leather bag, and I thought, you can't carry that, so I gave her a lift. We've got to get to know the locals, haven't we, Cassie, now we live here?'

She glanced pointedly at Cassie as she said it.

'She was so nice about Niall. She loves little children – especially babies. And she knew all about the old cottage that was here before this one. That's where that outhouse comes from she said. She was a real mine. In fact . . .'

Her mum hesitated, as she put the last of the bread in the bin.

'I've asked her to come for tea tomorrow. If I like her – and she's that good with babies – she could pop in sometimes and look after Niall if I want to go out. After all you're never that keen, are you?' This time she looked right at Cassie – meant to make her feel guilty.

But that wasn't what Cassie was feeling. What she was feeling was an emptiness, and a darkness and it was all lit by a black, greasy, candle.

'What was her name?' said Cassie quietly.

Because she'd already seen an old woman with a leather bag.

'She just said to call her Nanny Candle,' said her mum. 'Isn't that sweet?'

Before she went to bed, Cassie threw the plate with its mess of dirty wax out into the nettles, as far away from the house as she could. She heard it land. Then she scrubbed her hands clean under the tap and lay in her room with the light on, but she couldn't sleep. All she could think of was the old woman. Through the walls she could hear Niall crying, only if she listened carefully she could hear other crying too – faint, and far away. Crying that would stop, then start again, only it was never the same cry. It was always a different one.

She couldn't help thinking of the stone-floored kitchen and the iron range – she could almost see the shape of them rising out of the hard, lightbulb-lit room around her. At last, she pulled on her jumper and padded bare-foot along the dark passage to her mum's room. She felt safer there. There was a small lamp by her mum's bed – the light from it was soft and butter yellow – and her mum was holding Niall. He was asleep. Cassie climbed into the bed beside her.

'Please don't let that lady come,' she said. 'I dreamed about an old lady.'

Her mum shifted a little so that she could put one arm around Cassie.

27

It felt so warm, so comfortable.

'Don't be silly,' her mum said. 'You didn't see her. She was nice. Just a nice old lady.'

'She isn't nice, Mum,' said Cassie.

She looked up into her mum's face. 'Can we move away?' she said quietly. 'I don't like it here.' And she began to cry.

Her mum's face hardened and she took her arm away from Cassie. She still held on to Niall though.

'Well, you're going to have to learn to like it,' her mum said firmly. 'Because it's all that we've got, and that's an end of it.'

Large, wet tears welled up in Cassie's eyes and rolled down her cheek onto the pillow. But her mum didn't put her arm round her again.

It was just after three o'clock the next afternoon that the old woman came.

Cassie had tried everything she could think of to stop it happening, to make her mum change her mind, but none of it had worked. Short of actually running away there was nothing she could do, and she couldn't do that. So she waited, and now the woman was there, sitting at the little table her mum had laid.

But was it the same woman as in the dream?

Cassie couldn't say. She kept stealing looks at her, trying to decide, but she just couldn't say.

At last her mum said, 'Don't stare, Cassie!' And then she said, 'I'm sorry, Nanny. Cassie's left her manners somewhere else today.'

It wasn't the sort of thing her mum normally said – and if she'd said 'Nanny' once, she'd said it a dozen times. 'Nanny, would you like some tea?' 'Nanny, would you like some cake?' It sounded so false to Cassie, but the woman just smiled each time and took the tea and took the cake, and looked at Cassie and smiled some more.

'Lovely little baby brother you've got,' she said.

'His name's Niall,' said Cassie flatly.

'Oh, I know that, poppet, your mum told me. And I bet you love him to bits, don't you?' She turned to Cassie's mum. 'You know, dear, if ever you wanted me to stop by and look after him for a while, I'd never mind. It would be a nice treat for me, lovely little boy like that.' And she leaned forward and pinched Niall's cheek.

Her mum smiled. She picked up the empty teapot from the table and made for the little kitchen.

'I'll just go and get some more tea, and maybe we can talk about that.'

'I'll get it,' said Cassie quickly, but her mum had already gone, and there was just her and the woman.

The woman carefully sipped at her cup of tea, put it tidily down on the saucer and looked at Cassie. Only this time it wasn't the same woman who had sat there only the moment before.

It was someone else completely.

It was like a bad dream slowly blossoming in front of Cassie – the old lady in the dream and this other lady were both there at the same time sitting in the same chair – one face over the other – both talking at her.

'You lit it then,' the woman from the dream said.

Cassie stared at her open-mouthed. She felt giddy and sick – could taste the dirty wax on her tongue. Could smell it in the air mixed with the tea and the cake – all stale and fatty.

The woman smiled at her, and Cassie had seen that smile before.

'Nanny always leaves a little candle out to light her way back home,' the woman said.

She put a boney finger to her throat and Cassie saw on the white of her puckered skin, there underneath the collar of her dress, a livid blue and black bruise. It went on a slant all the way round her neck.

'Hangman did that for me, dearie,' she said. 'Hardly fair, when all I do is take those girls' little worries away. Their little mistakes.'

Looking slyly at Cassie, she picked up her cup and

sipped at it again. Only suddenly it was the lady who'd come for cake who was looking at her.

'You all right, poppet? You look all pale,' she said.

And then it wasn't her any more, it was that other face. Cold and heartless.

'Like your mummy's little mistake,' it said.

Cassie glanced at Niall sitting propped in his chair.

'Take him too, if you like? Put him in my bag of bricks, and that'll be the end. Nanny make it all better. You'll see.'

Cassie stuffed her hands over her ears to shut the words out, and what actually happened next she couldn't say, but her mum was there and the table was all turned over and the old lady who'd come for tea was standing pale-faced against the wall, flapping her hands at Cassie, trying to keep her off.

And then, Cassie was alone in the little room among the broken cups and dropped cake, listening to Niall crying from the passage and her mum showing the woman out of the door, saying over and over again how sorry she was. How really, really sorry she was. And when the woman had gone, her mum had stormed back in, face blanched white – Cassie had never seen her so angry. Niall was yelling blue murder in her arms, and Cassie couldn't begin to explain any of it, because her mum wouldn't listen – said Cassie had done it all on purpose just to hurt her. Wouldn't listen even when Cassie tried to tell her that Nanny Candle was going to come for Niall. That only made it worse.

And she was so scared.

Her mum didn't talk to her, wouldn't even look at her, for the rest of the day – not even a kiss at bedtime – and Cassie went to bed unloved and alone.

And then the power went off again.

She lay frightened and alone in the dark listening to her mum moving around by torchlight, singing to Niall to shush his crying. Then her mum had gone to bed and everything was quiet and dark. Cassie must have slept too, because when she opened her eyes the moon had moved round and its light was coming through the window onto her pillow. But it didn't shine on her bedroom. It shone on a kitchen with an iron range and a flagstone floor, and a candle flickering darkly on a shelf. She could smell its wax.

There was a bag and two bricks on the table, and through Cassie's headphones, loose and tangled on her pillow, she heard a whispering voice.

'. . . Nanny make it all better . . .'

Even as she watched, the latch on the kitchen door began to lift.

She had to wake her mum. But she knew her mum wouldn't believe her.

As the door began to open, Cassie slipped from her bed and hurried along the passage. Behind her in the dark she could hear the sound of Nanny Candle's buttoned boots on the stone floor. Hear the sound of Nanny Candle picking up the bag and the bricks. Noiselessly, Cassie crept into her mum's room. If she hid Niall, Nanny Candle wouldn't be able to find him. She could keep him safe.

The baby was asleep in the cot. He didn't so much as stir as she lifted him out. He smelled of warmth and milk, and biscuits and vanilla, and his hair was soft like down. She could feel it against her face. Why had she never done this before? She wrapped his blanket around him and carried him to the back door. There was a place to hide there – under the back steps. Nanny Candle wouldn't find them there.

Cassie carried him out into the cool dark and crouched with him under the steps. Held him to her. But he began to stir.

'Shh . . .' she said urgently. 'She'll hear you . . .'

But the baby began to make small waking sounds.

'No, no, no,' she said quickly. There was a rising panic in her voice. 'No, no, don't cry. Don't cry, or she'll find you.'

She could hear the sound of Nanny Candle coming.

As Niall began to cry, Cassie folded the corner of the blanket over his mouth and held it there, pressed it down.

'Ssshh . . . Ssshh . . .' she whispered, over and over again, rocking him in her arms until finally, he made no sound at all.

The boy blinked.

He was only then aware again of the platform and the lantern on the ground – because all that had as good as stopped while the old man was talking. He'd been watching Cassie, wanting to tell her not to fold the blanket over Niall's face. But slowly the world became real and dark about him.

'That was a horrible story,' he said.

'Do you think so?' the old man answered cheerfully.

He reached into his raincoat pocket and brought out a biscuit, bent down and held it out to the dog. The boy could see the little black nose, all shining and wet in the light of the lantern, the pink tongue and the white teeth.

'He's a lovely little dog, is Toby,' said the old man. 'Goes everywhere with me, he does, he's my

little shadow. You want to give him a biscuit?' he chirruped. 'He'll be your friend for life if you give him a biscuit.'

But the boy could still see the blanket and the baby's face.

The man reached into his pocket and handed him a small piece of broken biscuit.

'I keep them in my pocket,' he said. 'Because I know he likes a biscuit, but then, who doesn't like a biscuit?'

Shaking the image away, the boy took the biscuit and offered it to the little dog. He could feel its breath and warm tongue against his fingers. The biscuit made him think of the smell of the pet shop on the high street – all vanilla bones and bird meal.

'We haven't got a dog,' he said. 'My mum's allergic.'

'Well, you go on,' said the man. 'You make as much of a fuss of him as you want and it will help pass the time for you. He'll like it too. Look at him, happy as happy.'

The boy rubbed the dog's back and it wagged its tail. It looked up at him for more each time he stopped. Then it hoovered up the last of the crumbs, and cocked its head – all bright eyed and hopeful for more.

'It wasn't real,' the boy said. 'That story wasn't real.'

He didn't know why he'd said that. Maybe because in some way it had felt – still felt – real. As though there was a girl called Cassie, was a candle and a bag of bricks.

The man looked amused – like an elderly uncle who'd told a joke. He pursed his lips.

'What's real is what we believe,' he said. 'It's like lies – if you believe it when you tell it, it's not a lie, is it? You might be mistaken, but that doesn't make it a lie. Something can be in a story, and still be real – if you believe it.'

'Well, I don't,' the boy said. 'And I don't want to hear another one, thank you very much.'

The man smiled a friendly smile, took out a big coloured handkerchief and blew his nose noisily, then wiped his mouth on the hanky and put it away.

'I'm glad I came along,' he said brightly. 'Couldn't have you sit here all on your own in the dark, could we?'

The boy looked along the platform at the light of the lamps and the rails diminishing into that darkness.

'What time does the train come, do you know?'

'Depends what they're doing,' the man said thoughtfully. 'If they're doing ballast or tamping, it

37

will be one thing, and if they're putting in a new rail it'll be another.'

'Yeah, well, when's it come?'

'Like I said, it depends what they're doing. You should listen.'

'I was listening,' the boy said.

'No,' the man said. 'Listen – not to me, to the rails. You can always hear when a train's coming long before you see it. The rails start hissing – and that's the train, see? If you put a penny on the track the hissing will jump it off before the train comes. You should listen to the rails,' he said, pointing with the lead towards the track. 'That's what we used to do. That's the way you know when a train's coming.'

'It's going to come soon though, isn't it?'

'Oh, there's always a train going to come soon,' the man said. 'That's why you have to listen to the rails. ''Cause there's a train coming, and a train coming . . .'

His voice trailed off.

'. . . And a train coming –

TO GET YOU!'

He lurched towards the boy, and the boy was up and off the bench.

'What the—'

But the man wasn't looking at him, he was laughing at his joke, patting the scruffy little dog.

'We made him jump, didn't we, Toby? Made him jump proper. "Train coming to get you," we said.'

He looked up at the boy, his face creased in mirth.

'Stupid . . . !' the boy said.

'Well, there's no need for language,' the man said, his face suddenly falling. 'It was just a little joke.'

'Well, it wasn't funny,' the boy said sharply.

'Well. I don't know,' the old man said, his voice and face all offended. 'Come along here to keep you company, make sure you don't come to any harm, and that's what I get in return – language. I don't know at all.'

'I'm sorry,' the boy said. 'You just made me jump.'

'I was trying to make you laugh!' the man answered.

He looked about him, still offended.

'I'm sorry,' the boy said again.

'Well,' the man said.

He took out the handkerchief again, wiped his mouth, and put it away. Then he looked up into the boy's face.

'You sit down,' he said in a conciliatory way.

The boy sat down.

The little dog rested its head on the boy's knee. He could feel its warmth through his jeans. He stroked its ears.

'It's the dark, isn't it?' said the old man, and it seemed to the boy that there was kindness in his voice, as though perhaps he knew that that joke hadn't been the right thing to play. 'You don't like the dark much, do you, son? Well, none of us like the dark very much, that's why we have lights.' He tapped the lantern with his foot. 'Wouldn't go anywhere without my light. Tell you what, I'll tell you a story about lights. Nice, bright lights.'

'I don't want a story,' the boy said.

The man looked at him and smiled again.

'Course you do,' he said. 'We all like a nice little story about lights.'

And it happened again, the platform fading and the sound of the old man's voice becoming something else – not a story, but a real girl in a real hall by a real front door.

The Security Light

Jess's mum was wearing perfume and a burgundy-red dress, and the shoes she said didn't fit but looked nice.

'You'll be OK on your own, won't you?' she asked as she buttoned her coat. 'It's not as though dad and me go out that often, is it? And it is a Halloween party.'

'I'll be fine,' said Jess. 'Really. I've got stuff to do for Friday anyway.'

She didn't like it when her mum fussed.

'You're sure you don't want me to put something in on the timer for you?'

'No, I'll be fine,' said Jess again. 'Go on, you have a good time.'

'And you won't wait up, will you?' said her mum checking her hair in the mirror. 'It'll be late before we're back.'

Her dad gave Jess a kiss and picked up the car keys.

'If you get bored, don't chew the furniture,' he said.

They closed the front door.

Jess stood for a moment, then wandered into the kitchen and flicked the kettle on. She leaned against the worktop looking at her reflection in the patio doors while she waited for the water to boil. It was dark outside and the glass of the doors was like a black mirror. She couldn't see the little yard at all, only her reflection with the cupboards behind her and the kettle on the side.

She didn't like being on her own – never had. It wasn't that she didn't like the house, it was the emptiness of being on her own in it that she didn't like.

She didn't like being alone.

She didn't like the idea of Halloween either – what was put in a grave was meant to stay there. She didn't like thinking about what might come out of one – not that anything ever could.

All the tricking and treating was over for the night – the little boys and little girls, costumed and torch-lit, had been given sweets and were back home now, safe indoors. No one else was going to come knocking, which was just how Jess wanted it.

The water boiled. She made herself a drink, then brought her mum's sewing machine in from the front room and set it up on the table. Pulling the fabric and things she needed from her school bag, she spread them all out. When she'd done, she sat down with her headphones in and began cutting out paper patterns and pinning them to the cloth. As she worked she'd glance up and see her reflection looking back at her from the black mirror of the patio doors – like another girl working at another table, the kitchen light pulled low.

Every now and again the security light in the yard outside flicked on, but there was never anything there. It did it all the time. Her dad said it was the branches of next door's tree getting in the way, so he'd cut them right back, but the light still came on. It only took a cat, he said. The light flooded the yard and when it did Jess couldn't see herself in the glass any more, only the bin and the washing line, and the high back wall with the door that opened onto the alley where the garages were.

It was an unforgiving light.

The colours it made were too bright, the shadows too black – as sharp-edged as any razor. It looked all wrong – like a photograph of the yard, not the real thing. It hung there for a moment behind the patio doors, all bright and sharp, then the light would go out with a little *pik* noise. Everything would fade into darkness, and there would be her reflection again in the black mirror, cloth and scissors in hand, staring back at her as she looked out.

That light made the house feel even more empty. Made her feel even more alone.

Once or twice, the kitchen light gave a little flicker as though the bulb or the power was about to go, and she'd pause what she was doing and look up at it. But then the flickering would stop.

For a long while she was engrossed in what she

was doing – cutting and pinning, trying to feed the cloth through the machine without breaking the needle on the pins. But then something made her look up. All she could hear was the music in her ears. She pulled one of the headphones out and listened – perhaps it had been the phone, and she'd missed it. The house was quiet, just the sounds of the fridge and the boiler. But as she looked back down at the table she caught sight of her reflection and just for a moment, no more than a blink of an eye, she thought she saw something move behind it – something that drew itself away, backwards into the dark. She felt her heart skip a beat, and in the same moment the security light flicked on with its hard white light – but the yard was empty, even the door at the back was shut.

She sat staring, her eyes fixed on the sharp black shadows and the false bright colours, not sure at all what she could have seen.

Then *pik*. The light went out.

Unsettled now, she took her other headphone out and sat looking at the black of the glass – at her reflection staring impassively back at her as though it knew something that she didn't. She was almost certain she'd seen a movement. Wondering if it might have been something on the side behind her, she turned round and as she did all the lights in the house flickered once and went out. The fridge shuddered to a halt and she was left in complete darkness. Everything that made a sound had stopped. Even the heating. She sat for a moment in the silence waiting for it all to come back on again, but it didn't.

It was so quiet. So dark.

She craned her head to see up, on top of the cupboards. Even the little light on the internet box had gone out.

There was a small torch kept in the cutlery drawer behind her. She pushed her chair back and fumbled in the darkness until she found it. When she turned it on it gave out a thin little light, barely enough to see her hand by. The batteries were almost done. She shook it hard, but it didn't make a difference. The torch just seemed to make the darkness even darker. She felt her way along the worktop to the light switch by the door – clicked it on and off – but nothing happened. Then, bumping the table in the dark, she took the chair she'd sat on out into the hall and put it under the meter cupboard by the door. Her dad did that when a fuse had gone, but she'd never actually seen what it was he did next, and when she lifted up the flap of the cupboard and held the little beam of light to it, there was just a row of white and black buttons. She couldn't see anything that was 'off'.

But now she was on the chair she was on a level

with the little window above the front door and she could see outside. There weren't any lights on in the street either. She got off the chair. The torch made a tunnel of dark around her as she went up the stairs. She pushed open her mum and dad's door and, clambering over their bed, she looked out of the big window onto the street below. There wasn't a light to be seen anywhere. She pressed her face to the glass and peered both ways, her breath fogging the cold window. But all she could see was darkness and the silhouettes of rooves against the lighter dark of the sky.

She sat for a moment on the corner of the bed deciding what to do. She didn't want to stay up all alone in the dark house – and she'd get cold too with the heating off. Her iPod was downstairs though. If she was going to go to bed, she'd need that. She'd trodden on her phone and until she got that fixed that's all she'd got left for music.

She went back down the stairs, the torch beam getting weaker with every step until worse than useless. It gave out completely as she reached the bottom. She groped her way along the wall to the kitchen then, hand outstretched, felt for the table.

Out in the yard the security light went on.

It was so bright after the dark of the house.

She stood like a rabbit in a headlight, looking at

the brilliance of the empty yard – at the knife-sharp shadows and the kitchen lit up all around her.

She took a step away from the windows, stood with her back to the worktop, her eyes fixed on the yard, looking at every shadow, every dark place, watching for something to move.

Pik.

The yard faded into blackness.

It was dark only for moments. Then the light came on again, harder, brighter. The darkness it left, deeper, blacker.

It shouldn't be doing that.

She jumped as the phone behind her on the side glowed, buzzed and began its little xylophone ring. She snatched it up.

'Hello?'

From the other end of the line she could hear party noises – voices and laughter. Grown-ups acting like kids.

'Jessie, love.'

It was her mum.

Her mum was laughing too. Her voice faded as she turned away and shushed someone.

'There's no lights,' said Jess.

'You got any power?' her mum said. 'We've got none here. It's all gone dark.'

There was a whoop of laughter.

Her mum's voice faded again as she turned away from the phone.

'Sorry, love,' said her mum. 'You've got lights then, have you?'

'No,' said Jess sharply. 'There's no lights.'

She was looking out into the dark of the yard as she spoke, waiting for the security light to come on again.

'Mum?'

'Hang on love, your dad's saying something.'

The phone went muffled.

'Is Dad—'

'Your dad says to tell you there's a big torch down in the garage if you want one. It's by the back—'

'Is Dad there?' said Jess quickly. She was still looking at the yard. 'Can you ask him if the security light should be coming on? 'Cause that's what it's doing. It's freaking me out.'

She waited for her mum to answer. It took her a moment to realise that she couldn't hear the noise of the party any more. She couldn't hear anything. She looked at the phone in her hand. The light on it had gone out.

'No!'

She slapped the phone against her other hand, but it didn't come on again.

The charger was plugged into the socket by the

50

kettle. She put the phone in the cradle. Nothing happened, and only then did she realise that it wouldn't. She was trying to make it do something – anything – when the security light came on again behind her. This time out of the corner of her eye she saw something move – a shadow passed across the cupboards – as though something had crossed in front of the light. It was there and gone. She turned quickly round and looked.

The yard was empty.

Pik.

The light went out.

It came on again almost straight away. She stared. The door in the wall was open just a crack. Had it really been shut before? She couldn't say now whether it had or not. It could have been like that the whole time and she'd only just noticed.

Then the light went out, and everything went dark.

The house was silent.

There was a pair of curtains on a rail above the patio doors, but Jess never closed them. The edge of the rail was all worn and rough, and the runners caught if she tried. But now she pulled at the curtains in the dark, dragging them across the rail. They snagged and stuck. She gave them a tug and just as they closed the light went on again.

She couldn't see into the yard at all now – couldn't see if there was anyone there or not, and suddenly she wasn't sure if behind the curtains the patio doors were even locked. She pushed her hand through the gap, half-fearful that someone would catch hold of it, but the door was locked. She pulled her hand back and stood very still, holding her breath, looking at the light, all pale and translucent through the cloth of the curtains.

She was waiting for a shadow to move across it.

Pik.

The light went out.

There was a simple explanation – that's what she told herself. She'd just spooked herself, it was no more than that. Her dad would know what it was. If he were here, her dad would go and get the big torch from the garage. That's all she had to do – just go and get it – only that meant going out into the dark yard.

Or, she could go upstairs and wait. It wouldn't be long and her mum and dad would be home.

She felt her way out into the hall, stopped at the bottom of the stairs and listened. The house was so quiet. She could almost feel the emptiness of it pressing against her skin.

From the dark of the kitchen she heard a noise – like a tap on the glass of the patio doors. She froze, and listened again. It was just the handle going back into place where she'd tried to turn it.

But then, she heard the sound again, and this time she didn't wait. She got to the top of the stairs. Stopped and listened.

The house was silent.

She climbed fully clothed into her bed and, pulling the duvet up around her, lay there in the dark, eyes wide open, listening to the empty house. Down in the yard the security light flicked on. The spill of brightness lit up her ceiling and the wall above her head. It pulled shadows out of the corners of the room, making monsters of her coat, her bag, her shoes. Then *pik* it went out again.

She drew her knees up to her chest and made herself as small as she could as the light flicked on and off.

And then it stopped.

It went out and didn't come back on. It was just dark.

She began to count.

She'd got to one hundred and sixty and still the light hadn't come back on. She felt a wave of relief fill her, like warmth. Her fingers had been gripping the duvet tight, but now they relaxed, and she lifted her head up and looked at the empty room.

There was a light beneath the gap under her door.

The downstairs lights had come back on. She

threw the duvet off and went out onto the landing. The stair light was off, but at the bottom of the stairs she could see the hall and the front door – all the downstairs lights were on.

'Yes!' she said.

And then something made her stop. Something that was not right.

There were no other lights on at all. Not on the stairs, not on the landing. Everything was dark. Frowning, she flicked at the switch beside her on the wall. Nothing happened. Through her mum and dad's open door she could see the big window onto the street. See the silhouetted rooves of dark houses against the lighter dark of the sky.

There were no lights on anywhere, except downstairs.

She stood at the top of the stairs and looked again at the carpet in the hall – it was like a photograph she'd never seen before, all bright and sharp in a hard light.

With a click the downstairs lights went off, and everything below her was dark again.

She felt her stomach tighten.

She stood stock still, straining to hear any sound.

From somewhere downstairs she heard a noise – small and short, as though something had been knocked against.

And then another.

Someone was moving about in the darkness.

One hand on the wall behind her, Jess began backing away towards her door. As she reached it, she heard from the darkness the creak of the bottom stair. She pulled her door closed as quietly as she could, stood inside gripping the handle shut, her ear pressed against the wood, listening.

From along the landing, she heard a click as the mirror light in the bathroom turned on and then off.

Then the landing light clicked on.

There was not another light in the whole street, but one by one the lights in the rooms along the landing were being turned on and off, each time closer.

She held her breath.

As though it was being tested, she felt the handle of her door begin to turn against her grip. She stifled a whimper, and held the handle more tightly. The turning stopped.

At her feet, light spilled beneath the crack of the door. Then there was the click of the landing switch, and the light went out, leaving only dark.

She stood, absolutely rigid, listening for the slightest sound from the silence.

But the sound when it came wasn't from the landing on the other side of the door, it was from the darkness of the room behind her.

It was a laugh that wasn't human – a mocking laugh, full of envy and spite from the cold empty soil of a grave.

She pulled wildly at the door and the handle, but fixed by some force she could not overcome, the door wouldn't open now—

wide-eyed she slowly turned to look behind her,

and in the dark of her little room, the bedside light clicked on.

The boy looked uneasily out into a dark that had become railway tracks. Imagined it all being lit by a sudden blaze of light – the bushes and the branches leaping out stark and shadowed then, pik, it all fading to darkness.

He felt as though the man was waiting for him to say something, maybe waiting for him to say he was frightened. But he wasn't going to say that.

'Sorry,' the old man said. 'Did you say something?'

'I think I'll go and ring my dad,' said the boy.

He got up and walked down the platform away from the man. Beyond the last lamp everything was dark, so he stopped at the furthest edge of the weak pool of light it cast. The air was cold against his face. He could feel it filling the hollows of his clothes.

He pulled the phone from his pocket, willing the thing to come on when he pressed the button, but it didn't. Not even the screen lit up this time. He felt stupid having walked down there only to walk back, so he held the phone to his ear all the same and started talking, loudly enough to be heard, as though there was someone at the other end.

'Yeah,' he said, turning on his heel and looking back down the platform at the bench. 'Just waiting for it now.' He pretended to listen. 'No, not on my own – there's an old man with his dog. Could you put Mum on?'

He wasn't sure why he was doing it – it was false comfort – but when he'd done, he slipped the phone back into his pocket and stood for a while under the light, but there was only darkness beyond it and that made him think of the little back yard and the darkness that was left when the light went out. So he walked slowly back towards the bench.

The man looked up.

'Been for a little constitutional, have you?' he said. 'Got to keep warm on a night like this.'

'I was just talking to my dad.'

The man looked right at him.

'You should have given him to me,' he said. 'I could have told him I was waiting with you. Ring him back,' he said, almost silkily. 'Go on, you ring him back, and I'll tell him it's all right 'cause I'm here. All tickety-boo here.'

'No,' the boy said.

'It's no trouble.'

'No!'

The boy said it louder than he'd meant to.

'No,' he said again, more evenly. 'He's just got to go out.'

'Suit yourself,' the man said, and he looked at the little dog. 'Course,' he said, almost as though it was an afterthought, 'I wouldn't trust one of them things myself. Never trust anything with a battery, that's what I say.'

He looked up at the boy and smiled.

'Never know when they'll let you down,' he said softly.

He leaned sideways so that he could get to his other pocket and, fumbling in it, took out a pepper-mint and popped it into his mouth. The boy could smell the cool warmth of the mint, hear the click of it against his teeth.

'Want a mint?' the old man said brightly.

He held out the packet, and the boy took one, sat back down on the bench and stuffed his hands deep into the warmth of his pockets.

The boy realised he must have looked so stupid pretending on the phone, and that the man had guessed that it wasn't working. And he didn't like the thought of that.

'How old is your little dog?' he said.

They were words just to move the moment on.

'What, little Toby?'

The man looked down at the grubby scruff of fur, and took a long breath in.

'Ooooh, don't know that,' he said. 'But lucky for you him and me coming along, wasn't it? Look at us three, chatting away like old friends – you and me and Toby. Bit of luck that was. I like a nice bit of luck.'

He settled himself comfortably back against the bench and when he spoke again, it took the boy a moment to realise that it wasn't a conversation he was starting.

It was another story, he could almost see it – a man sitting by a boy in a car.

Your Lucky Day

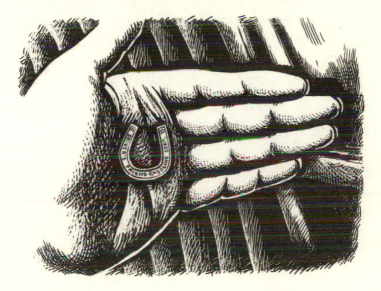

Sam and his dad didn't normally drive that way home.

'I want to show you something,' said his dad.

But he wouldn't say what it was. He just grinned at Sam, the grin getting wider each time Sam asked him. Finally, up by the old factories, he pulled over onto the grass verge, grinned at Sam again, turned off the engine and got out.

'Come on,' he said. 'Come and see.'

Only, there was nothing there to see – just a car parked up by the old wire fencing a bit further along the scrub of grass.

A big red car.

His dad started walking towards it, and then Sam realised that's what his dad wanted him to see – the car.

It was an old American one, left-hand drive and big as a fairground ride – all red paint and polished chrome with tail fins, and lights at the back large as dinner plates. Even the walls of the tyres were painted, and they were spotless white. It was the sort of car his dad had always wanted.

'You don't get monsters like this any more,' his dad said as he walked round it. 'That's pure rock and roll, Sam.'

It was just parked there on the grass at the side of the road.

'Wasn't here yesterday,' said his dad. 'You have to be quick in this life.'

Sam put his face to the glass of the window and peered in. It was like a picture from a glossy magazine – the steering wheel all ivory white, and a big chrome radio with dials gleaming in the middle of the dash. The seats were red leather, all creased and worn. The rear-view mirror, large as a shoe box. Taped inside the windscreen was a piece of paper with a mobile number and a price in thick felt pen.

'You like it?' said his dad.

He grinned again, a really big grin this time, and before Sam could answer, he'd put his hand in his coat pocket and taken out an old key fob, unlocked the door and got in. He pulled the sheet of paper off the windscreen and screwed it up.

Sam stared at him with his mouth open. 'What you doing?' he said.

'You get a chance like this once in a lifetime, Sam,' his dad said. 'I wasn't going to let it slip me by.'

He turned the key and hit the starter. The engine coughed, missed as though it were making up its mind whether to start or not, then growled into life.

'You bought it?'

'Rock and roll, Sam,' said his dad.

He leaned across and opened the passenger door.

'What about the other one?' asked Sam, looking back along the verge at their old Fiesta.

'We're picking your mum up, dropping her off here, then taking this one to Frank's. He's going to have a look at it for me. Give it the once over.'

He stroked the ivory white steering wheel.

'Rock and roll,' he said again.

His dad was big on rock and roll.

Sam got in beside him, steering wheel all on the wrong side. The door was big and heavy, and the red leather trim came loose as he closed it. He pushed it back on its studs.

'Does Mum know?'

His dad grinned at him.

'Course she knows.'

His dad put the car into gear and it rolled forward and sank down, like a big sponge mattress, off the grass and onto the hard tarmac of the road.

Sam looked about him at the inside of the car. It wasn't half as smart as it had seemed through the window. The roof lining was all stained and the trim shabby. The leather of the seats was worn and soiled, and the wide-bench back seat had sunk in where people had used it. You could see the shape of where they'd sat. But his dad didn't seem to notice any of it.

They picked up his mum from the corner by her

work. She was already there, like a kid waiting for a present. She made Sam get in the back and even though it was cold she sat in the front with the window down and her hair blowing everywhere, making up stories about the places in America the car must have been – all the high school proms and the big pink dresses, and the baseball games and the letterman jackets. Shopping malls and gas stations. She loved it. She loved it all.

She didn't see the shabbiness of it either – didn't see the wrongness of it all.

'Rock and roll!' shouted Sam's dad and he turned on the radio loud as it would go, and there was some sixties rock and roll song playing, and his mum and dad stared at each other, then burst out laughing and sang along at the top of their voices, his mum leaning her arm out of the window with the wind going through her hair like she was Marilyn Monroe.

But Sam sat in silence on the back seat looking out of the window at the people turning their heads to watch the big red car go by, and he didn't like it.

He didn't like the long, cold, empty seat next to him – it was wide enough for four – and the red leather was all worn and stained. And he didn't like the chipped chrome buckle and the stained webbing of the seatbelt. And most of all, he didn't like that shape in the seat next to him, because it was like there was a person sitting there that he couldn't see, riding in the car with them.

There was a smell about it too that he couldn't place. It was mixed in with the smell of the leather and damp carpet – it was stale and sickly – and he just couldn't place it. It was something that made him think of the shops.

His fingers folded into the crack at the back of the seat, and they touched something cold and hard down there, like a coin. He closed his fingers round it and fished it out.

For a moment he wasn't sure what it was. It wasn't a coin. It was covered in muck and fluff. He wiped it clean. It was a little metal horseshoe, like a lucky charm. He held it up to the window. It had words on it in worn, green paint – 'Driver's Friend Gasoline Corp' on one side and 'Your Lucky Day' on the other. They were the same words as on the leather key fob hanging from the ignition beneath the ivory white steering wheel. He could see now there was a loop at the top of the horseshoe and a torn bit of leather on the fob. It must have come off sometime, was probably how it had found its way down the back of the seat. He squirmed round in the seatbelt and put his fingers into the crack again, but there was nothing else there, just dirt and old Hershey Bar wrappers.

He looked again at the Driver's Friend horseshoe in the palm of his hand. The painted words were chipped and worn, and even as he looked at it he felt a chill come over him.

He could see his mum and dad laughing and smiling, could hear the radio and his mum singing along, but it was like it was two cars now and he was in the other one, and everything in that car was cold and still and silent.

And there was someone else in it.

He glanced uneasily at the long emptiness of the seat next to him, at the shape like a back pressed deep into the worn leather.

'I said "petrol".'

He looked up.

His dad was smiling at him in the rear-view mirror. The big car was swinging off the road and onto a garage forecourt. It sank down on its suspension as it went over the bump of the kerb, and then it was next to the pump and his dad was getting out. For a while Sam's mum sat in the car with him while his dad filled the tank, then she got out too and stood leaning against the front wing. Sam knew she was pretending to be standing at some gas station at the side of a freeway.

He didn't like being alone in the car. It was disturbingly quiet and cold and still. He could see his mum through the windscreen, hear the wash of the petrol going into the tank, but it felt like he was in that other car. He started to undo his belt and as he sat forward, for a moment – no more than a blink – it was as though someone was looking at him out of the rear-view mirror – a face he didn't know. Then it was gone and there was just the cold empty car and the sound of the petrol going into the tank. The glove box in the dashboard dropped open all on its own, it fell against the dash and the sound of it made him jump. He unclipped the belt and got out of the car.

But that cold feeling got out with him. It was there on the forecourt like a presence standing just behind him. It didn't go away. It made the skin on the back of his neck crawl. It got back into the car with him too when they drove off. It was there in the empti-ness next to him on the seat.

They dropped his mum off at the other car like his dad said they would.

'I'll go with Mum,' Sam said.

But his dad wanted him with him – 'me and my boy'. So that's where Sam went. To Frank's house.

Frank drove lorries. When he wasn't driving lor-ries, he fixed cars.

'So what do you think?' said Sam's dad all smiles and proud of what he'd bought.

They'd pulled up outside Frank's house and Frank had fetched a big lamp from his garage and crawled underneath the red car and poked inside.

'Whole front's new,' he said. 'And all the glass.'

'That's a good thing, "new", isn't it?' said Sam's dad.

That wasn't what Frank had meant. He pulled a face. He shone the big lamp down into the dark places behind the engine, ran his finger along the line of a rough welded seam so they could see it. It ran all the way round, like stitches in a wound.

'So?' said Sam's dad. He sounded less certain now.

'So – it's been in a smash,' said Frank. 'That whole front's new – all of it. The chassis's not straight either. You've got to hit something a real whack to do that kind of damage. I'd have nothing more to do with it, if I were you. If that's not been in a fatal,' he said, 'I'm a monkey.'

Sam and his dad got back into the car and drove off.

His dad didn't say anything until they were nearly home. Then, as though he was talking to himself as much as talking to Sam, he said, 'Yeah, well Frank doesn't know everything, does he? That's just guessing, what he says. It's not that it doesn't drive OK.' He looked sideways at Sam. 'It's not as though it doesn't drive OK,' he said again, louder this time, 'and it's all new. There's nothing wrong with the way it drives.'

He patted the dashboard.

'You're a beauty,' he said. Then he smiled again. 'Rock and roll, Sam.'

More felt than seen, behind them on the back seat Sam thought something had moved. Like someone shifting in the seat. He looked up into the rear-view mirror, he couldn't help it, but the back seat was empty. Just worn shapes in the leather.

When they got home, his mum asked if Frank had liked the car, and his dad said 'yeah' – that the whole front was brand new. But he didn't say it like Frank had said it. He said it like it was good, and he'd given Sam a look. His mum had been so pleased – how could Sam say anything that would spoil it for her?

So he didn't.

'I'm going to run a bath,' he said and he went upstairs.

He wanted to wash the smell of the car off him. He didn't even like to think of it, all red paint and chrome, parked in the road outside the house with the shapes of dead people in the empty seats. 'Been in a fatal', that's what Frank had said and Frank was always right about cars – that's what his dad used to say.

He emptied his pockets in his room, turned them out onto the side, and found the little horseshoe in amongst his money.

He stopped and looked at it.

'Your Lucky Day'.

Hadn't been lucky for the people in the car, had it?

He couldn't remember putting it in his pocket, and he didn't want it. It made him feel like he felt when he was in the car, like he'd felt at the garage – that there was somebody standing just behind him. In fact the feeling was so real that he turned round and looked at the empty bedroom just to be certain – at the curtains, and the wardrobe, and his school bag lying on the floor by his bed. It felt like it used to feel when he woke up in the night when he was small and thought there was someone there in the dark that he couldn't see.

He realised that he was holding his breath.

He put the horseshoe on his dresser – right at the back – covered it over with a scrap of paper so he wouldn't have to see it, then went to run his bath.

The bathroom wasn't very big. It was always cold. The steam from the taps filled it, misted the mirror over. He sat in his clothes on the laundry basket until the water had run. Then he got undressed and lay back in the bath with the condensation making little beads and rivulets down the paint on the cold walls.

The water was warm and comforting and he put the damp flannel over his face and closed his eyes.

Then, as certain as if he'd seen them step into the room, it felt as though there was someone else there. He snatched the flannel off his face, sat up and looked round, but it was just him in the water. Suddenly he felt very naked and alone in that cold little room. Something fell over on the glass shelf under the mirror. One of his mum's nail varnishes was rolling slowly towards the edge. He watched it roll and drop into the sink below. He didn't want to be on his own in there any more. He wanted to be downstairs with his mum and dad. He pulled the plug out and wrapped himself in a towel while the condensation made lines on the mirror, like someone running their finger down the glass.

He got dressed still damp, and then hesitating, took the horseshoe off his dresser and, going downstairs, threw it in the bin outside the back door. He felt better then. Felt better, until he woke in the night and could hear little sounds from the dark of the room – just every now and then, little taps and clicks like someone picking things up and putting them down again. He lay absolutely still in the dark, listening. Then the feeling was gone and everything was quiet. All he could hear were the comforting sounds of the house – the click of the meter by the stairs, and the boiler coming on.

His mum wasn't at work the next day, so she was there when he came down in the morning.

'What were you doing up last night?' she said.

He looked at her and shook his head.

'I wasn't up.'

She pulled a face as though it didn't matter anyway. 'I thought I heard you moving around.'

She put his cereal in a bowl on the table, and that's when he saw the little horseshoe. It was next to his spoon.

'I found it in the bin,' said his mum. 'Thought it might be yours and you didn't know it was there.'

'It's not mine,' he said. 'It was down the back of the seat in the red car.'

She looked at it. 'Well, you should keep it then,' she said. 'Lucky thing like that.'

But he didn't want to keep it, and it didn't feel lucky.

He couldn't put it in the bin again, not if his mum might see it there, she'd only take it out. So he took it off the table and put it in his pocket, but he knew what he was going to do with it.

When he came to the canal, he put his bag down

at the side of the bridge, took the horseshoe from his pocket and, not even looking at it, threw it as far as he could out into the water. It made a noise like a small stone – hardly even that – and it was gone, sideslipping as it sank through the dirty water into the thick, filthy ooze at the bottom.

He turned his back and walked away, and he felt happy like he couldn't remember ever feeling so happy before. He looked about him at the road and the buses, and the shops and the people and just smiled, then he started to run for the joy of it.

It was like that for him all day. He didn't think of the horseshoe again, didn't think of the big red car, not even once. He ran home at the end of school, came in at the back door and threw his bag down on the kitchen table.

His mum didn't look up and he knew at once that something was wrong.

She wanted to know if he thought it was some kind of joke, because if he did, he could clean it all up and see if he was still laughing afterwards.

He didn't know what she meant.

She was so angry.

'I thought you'd gone to the toilet in it,' she said. 'You might just as well have. All them clothes. Well, you're not getting new ones – I'm telling you that now.'

He couldn't begin to understand what she was talking about. It was something about his room. He didn't bother taking his coat off, he went straight up the stairs. His door was open and the drawer of the dresser pulled out. The floor around it was sopping wet – like filthy water had been poured all over it – it was still dripping through the bottom of the dresser. The whole thing stank like the canal.

All his clothes in the drawer were sodden with dirty water and smeared with thick, stinking muck. He simply couldn't understand how it had happened. He picked all his clothes out one by one with his finger tips and dropped them in a wet pile on the floor, and still he didn't understand how it could have happened, where it could have come from. Then something like a coin fell from one of the folds of wet cloth, and landed on the floor at his feet.

Only it wasn't a coin.

As certain of it as he was certain of anything, someone had come to stand behind him. They hadn't been there a moment before, but they were there now. He could feel the skin on the back of his neck begin to crawl, just like at the garage. He turned slowly round, but the room was empty.

His mum was at the door holding an old washing-up bowl.

'You can put it all in here,' she said, and the

moment she said it, the feeling went, it was just him and her and an empty room.

He tried to tell her that he'd thrown the horseshoe in the canal, but she thought he meant he'd thrown it in then fished it out and brought it home and put it all wet and filthy in the drawer – but that didn't make any sense. She wouldn't listen when he tried to tell her that she was wrong, she just talked over him and didn't give him a chance, then left him alone in the room to clear it all up.

She was still angry when his dad came home, and that made it worse because he found out then that they'd planned a treat for him – for all of them. They were going out in the big red car – going bowling. His dad had booked the lane and everything. They'd drive up and have burgers and chips—

and it was all spoilt now.

He tried to tell his dad what had happened, but his dad didn't want to listen either. He just knew that Sam had done something stupid and that was an end to it. Least said soonest mended. Only it wasn't Sam who had done it and it wasn't mended.

But his dad had booked the lane, and it would be a waste of money if they didn't go.

His mum didn't talk to him in the car – only his dad did – asking him if he was all right in the back, which he wasn't. His mum only spoke to his dad – in that 'nothing has happened, but I'm not talking to you' sort of way that she had when Sam had done something wrong. Then she put the radio on and opened the window.

Sam sat on the cold, long back seat and all he could do was think of what Frank had said, and the horseshoe.

He hadn't known what to do with it when he'd cleaned up the mess. But he thought that if he put it back – if he put it back down the crack in the car seat – then maybe everything would be all right. So that's what he'd done. When he'd got in, he'd shoved it back down – pushed it further still so that it wouldn't come out. He put the tips of his fingers in every now and then just to make sure it was still there.

Bowling was no fun. His dad tried to make all his usual jokes, but they didn't work because his mum wouldn't join in and finally even his dad gave up, and they played out the last games in a sulky silence just to get the thing over with and go home.

The big red car was waiting for them in the dark car park, all shining paint and gleaming chrome under the street lights. When Sam got in, sat on the cold worn leather of the back seat and put on his belt, he knew there was someone else already there in the dark.

The car had that smell again, stale and sickly. He

couldn't place it, but he was almost there, he knew that smell.

His dad drove the car out of the car park and Sam looked out of the window and watched the street lights go by – looked at his mum and dad lit by the glow of the dashboard. He just wanted to get home, to get out of the car. As he looked out he could see the reflection of his own face doubled against the window glass.

As they came to the long, straight stretch of the bypass, his dad glanced at his mum.

'Let's see what this monster can do,' he said.

From the back of the car Sam saw his dad settle himself into the seat as he dropped a gear and floored the pedal. With a growl the big car leaped forward and as it did Sam's seatbelt clicked undone. He closed it again, but it came open straight away, only this time as he put his hand down to close it, he gasped as he felt the cold fingers of someone else's hand brush against his in the dark and unclip the belt again.

'Mum!'

He tried to put the clip back, to hold it closed, but there was always another hand in the way. The car was absolutely flying.

It was flat out.

'Rock and roll!' shouted his dad.

'You be careful!' said Sam's mum and she reached out towards the dashboard as though suddenly she was afraid, and as she did the car lurched sideways, slewing across the road towards the big concrete pillars of the bypass bridge. She let out a scream, and in that moment Sam saw, doubled in the glass beside his own reflection, the grinning face of someone next to him in the dark of the back seat, and he realised what the smell in the car was.

It was just like the smell of meat in the butcher's shop.

As the man's voice trailed off, the dark on the platform became real again, seemed even darker than before.

For several moments, the boy thought he'd actually heard, could still hear, the dreadful smash of glass and metal, but there was nothing but silence. The only sound was of the old man shifting on the bench.

'Everybody needs company.'

The old man said it as though he hadn't told the story at all.

'Everyone needs someone to look after them,' he said. 'Your mum and dad, they look after you, don't they? You and that brother of yours. I bet he's a little tiger.'

The man laughed at the thought.

'Games you must get up to.'

He paused and looked up at the lamps.

'Them lights will probably go out soon,' he said. 'They do that, you know – turn the lights off to save a bit of money. That's why I've got my lantern. You won't get me caught with the lights going out. Not with my lantern.'

The boy didn't feel comfortable any more. He wanted the old man to stop talking. To go away.

'Do you live very far from here?' he asked.

He hoped the man might take the hint, but the man only looked at him and smiled. The boy wished he wouldn't keep smiling like that.

'Not far, but Toby likes a nice walk this time of night,' he said. 'Who doesn't like a nice walk?'

'Why do you walk along the railway?' the boy said. He could feel himself getting cross now. 'There's trains.'

'Not that many,' the man said. 'Besides, I was waiting for you to get off.'

He laughed.

'Sooner or later, someone always gets off. Then there's Toby and me and my lantern, and we can keep them company. Play my little game together.'

He didn't say anything more than that, just took a deep breath and looked contentedly down the platform and out into the dark. But the words hung *in the air like a hook, and the boy felt a sudden cold that was nothing to do with the night.*

'What game?' he said.

The old man leaned towards him.

'I'm going to have a nice bit of fish when I get in,' he said. 'See you safe on the train, and then have a nice bit of fish. What are you going to have when you get in – you going to have a nice bit of fish?'

It was so harmless a question, but behind it, that hook still hung in the air.

'You tell me what you're going to have, then,' the old man said. 'It's always nice thinking about a good hot plate of food when you're a bit parky.'

'I don't know.' The boy shrugged. 'Pizza?'

'That's Italian, isn't it?'

'Sort of.'

'I expect you'll be ready for your bed by the time you get in. Late hour like this. At least you've got your mum and dad waiting up for you. It's those kiddies who have to fend for themselves I feel sorry for. All that babysitting and stuff while their mums and dads are out gadding about – you ever do that? Do any of that babysitting stuff?'

'Sometimes,' he said.

Sometimes he did – he'd look after their neighbours' children. He never liked it. Once or twice his mum had got him to help out someone at her work.

The old man smiled.

'Got a story about that,' he said.

And as he began to speak, the world about the boy seemed to shift again.

Babysitting

It wasn't a house Sophie had ever babysat at before, but that wasn't such an unusual a thing. She had the people she'd do regularly and sometimes they'd recommend her to their friends – and that would be a new house. Even if that wasn't how tonight's people had got hold of her, then chances were they'd seen her card in the newsagent's window – she got jobs that way too – and that was always a new house. She hadn't spoken to these people though – her mum must have taken the call because the details were waiting for her on the pad by the phone where she could see them as soon as she came in from school. Her mum was on nights this week and whoever it was must have rung just as her mum was going out through the door because the writing was a complete scribble – Sophie would hardly have said it was her mum's at all – but the bits about the time and how to get to the place were clear enough, and that's all that she really needed. She peeled the note off the pad and stuck it on the fridge door while she made herself a mug of tea and got herself something to eat. Then she sorted out her bag, watched the clock round till it was time and set off.

It was still just about light.

She knew the road the house was on well enough – it had been on her paper round when she used to do one – but she didn't know the actual house at all.

As she remembered it, there wasn't one at the bottom of the road where the directions said there was – least not one she'd ever seen. The road just ended in a thick, high hedge, and nothing had been built there since. So she went down the road with the paper from the pad thinking that the directions her mum had written down had to be wrong. But when she got to the bottom of the road, she saw that they weren't.

There was a gap in the hedge and a rutted path behind it just like the directions said there would be. She'd never noticed the gap or the path before, but you can do that. Even in a place you think you know really well, there'll be something you won't see unless you look for it. Sophie stood for a moment wondering why she'd never noticed it before. The path disappeared between overgrown clumps of shrubs and bushes. But she couldn't see the house.

It had been raining in the day and the ruts in the path were filled with water. She picked her way between them. The path wound through the wet shrubs and bushes, and it wasn't long before she couldn't see the road any more, but she couldn't see the house either and she was just beginning to wonder whether she'd got this right or whether she should go back and try another way, when the garden opened out in front of her and she came to an uncut, tussocky lawn. There was an old stone fishpond with a sundial and behind that, the house. It was what the estate agents in the town would have described as 'a large Victorian villa in need of renovation'. It looked cold and uncared for, an ugly slab of a place with shutters to the windows and large panes of black glass. There were steps up to a painted front door with a fanlight above it and a brass loop in the wall that rang a bell which Sophie faintly heard answer from inside when she pulled on it.

She took a step back and waited.

For a while nothing happened. She was about to pull the loop again when she heard children's voices approaching the door on the other side, and something wooden being dragged along a hard floor. She could hear the voices bickering about whose turn it was to open the door. There seemed to be two of them.

She put her mouth to the door.

'Could you get your mum?' she said. 'Tell her it's Sophie. I'm the babysitter.'

There was a pause, then more scraping and bumping, and the door opened on a chain. The gap was wide enough for Sophie to see a brown-haired girl. The girl was standing on a chair so that she could reach the door lock, and there was a brown-haired boy peering from behind her. Sophie eyed them up quickly trying to gauge just how much trouble they were likely to be. They must have both been about seven. The girl was wearing a faded Minnie Mouse T-shirt and the boy a blue camouflage one with 'Captain Action' written across it.

'Could you get your mum or your dad?' she said.

The girl and the boy glanced at each other. Then the girl undid the chain, climbed down off the chair and moved it to one side so that she could open the door wider.

'They've already gone,' she said. 'But we knew someone would be coming.'

She had a prim voice – *private school*, thought Sophie – but for all that it sounded resigned and disappointed, as though being left alone wasn't something new, and Sophie felt sorry for her. The girl reached out, her hand was soft and warm, and taking hold of Sophie she drew her firmly in through the door. The boy closed it behind them, then he pushed past Sophie and, running over-excitedly down the hall, did a slide on the hard, polished floor in his blue-socked feet. Then he ran back and did the same thing the other way.

Little show-off, thought Sophie.

'Did they leave me a note or a number I can ring?' she asked.

The girl and the boy glanced at each other again.

'I don't think so,' said the girl.

Sophie ran the answer quickly through her head – there had to be a note somewhere. Probably in the kitchen, she'd find it later, but it wasn't a good start.

'I'm Sophie,' she said, dropping her bag onto the floor.

'I'm Lucy,' said the girl.

'And we're Tom,' said the boy.

There was something annoyingly babyish about the way he said it. As though no one had ever bothered correcting him, and he hadn't quite understood yet that there was only one of him.

He did another slide on the polished floor.

'Well,' said Sophie. 'What we'll do is look for a note, and if we can't find one we'll sort out when bedtime is and then work back from there.'

That's what she normally did, and it usually worked, but the girl had already seemingly lost interest in her. She'd wandered off into one of the other downstairs rooms.

Sophie followed her.

It was a large, high-ceilinged room with a worn green tartan carpet on the floor. There were big armchairs and sofas too – and they were worn and threadbare as well – and a sideboard and table, both polished and dark and heavy. It was a cold room – untidy, as though no one ever bothered to put things back after they'd used them. There were empty boxes of games on the floor with the contents tipped out and strewn around. In one corner was a flat-screen television, larger than at Sophie's house. It was the sort that costs a lot of money.

The girl flopped down on the sofa and pointed the remote at the flat screen, it came to life in a hiss of untuned static.

'What time do you go to bed?' said Sophie.

The girl didn't answer. She didn't even look at Sophie. The boy came in and flopped face down onto the cushions beside his sister. He wriggled over onto his back and, resting his head in her lap, lay looking at the fizzing, white screen – his blue-socked feet dangling over the arm rest.

'Well, I'll go and see if I can find a note,' said Sophie.

It was going to be a long evening.

Outside the light had almost faded.

She found the kitchen. It was wide and long – a mixture of expensive new and tatty old. But there was no note that she could see, not on any of the sides or stuck to the fridge. She began to wonder if there was something her mum had missed telling her, some instruction she hadn't written down. Her mum didn't like Sophie to ring her at work, but she'd just have to put up with it this time. Sophie went back into the hall, fished her phone out of her bag and dialled her mum. It took her a few goes before she realised there was no signal.

Sophie went back into the high-ceilinged room. The girl and the boy were still lying on the sofa watching the static-filled screen. They hadn't even bothered to find a station.

'Is there anywhere . . .'

She couldn't think over the sound of the static, and it struck her as rude of them not even looking at her – so she bent down, picked the remote up from the sofa and turned the screen off.

They both looked up.

'We were watching that,' they protested.

She didn't pay them any notice.

'Is there anywhere here I can get a signal?' she said.

The girl and the boy glanced at each other.

'You have to go upstairs,' said the girl, 'and hold the phone out of the top window, or go onto the roof.'

'Have you got a landline?'

They looked at each other again.

It was rather an annoying habit.

'No,' said the girl.

She reached up to take the remote out of Sophie's hand, but Sophie moved it away.

The girl frowned, and then her face brightened.

'If we let you turn the telly off,' she said. 'Will you play with us?'

Sophie looked down at the emptied and broken boxes of games strewn round the carpet.

'All right then,' she said. 'And while we're playing we'll sort out what we're going to do next.'

The boy scrambled off the sofa his face suddenly eager and interested.

'She's going to play with us!'

Sophie began picking up boxes trying to find one that was vaguely complete.

'No, not them,' said the boy, and he took the box out of her hand. 'We like playing chase. We chase—'

'And I catch,' said the girl.

The girl turned and giggling began running round the room, the boy chased after her. They clambered over the backs of the sofas and jumped down onto the cushions, then scrambled behind the chairs pushing them over and when they bumped into each other they'd flap at one another with their hands, then chase again, the circles getting smaller and faster – chair, sofa, cushions. At first it seemed just a bit babyish and stupid, but the more it went on the more disturbing it got.

'I think that's enough now,' said Sophie.

But they didn't pay her any attention, they just got

wilder – the boy hot and red-faced, kicking at the girl with his socked feet to keep her off him, and the girl breathless and pale pulling him to the ground. He tried to crawl away from her but she dragged him back by his leg and sat heavily on his chest, pinning his wrists to the floor and putting her mouth against his face as though she was going to bite it. Sophie didn't know if it was a pretend fight or a real one any more. Then, damp and breathless, the girl let go of the boy's wrists and sat back. She brushed her tangled hair out of her face, and let him push her off him. They lay panting against each other on the floor amongst the broken boxes of games looking up at Sophie.

Still lying on her back the girl said suddenly, 'What's your party trick?' The question caught Sophie by surprise but the girl didn't give her time to answer. 'Do you want to see mine?' she said. 'I can open my mouth really wide.'

She opened her mouth.

Sophie could see the white of her teeth, but it wasn't that wide at all.

Not to be outdone, the boy sat up. 'And we can open our eye really wide,' he said.

He put his finger to the skin below one eye and pulled it down a bit revealing a little line of red inside the lid.

'That's gross,' said Sophie.

He seemed pleased with the result.

'You shouldn't do that, though. You'll make your eye sore.'

She didn't feel like playing a game any more and wondered what she was going to do with them.

She didn't like them at all. Didn't like this house.

Maybe food was the answer.

'Have you eaten yet?' she said.

They shook their heads.

'Then come and show me what there is in the kitchen.'

They looked at each other again, but neither of them moved.

Sophie took a breath that was more an audible exercise of patience than anything else, and went back across the hall to the kitchen. She had to turn the light on now. She opened the first two cupboards she came to, but they were just plates and bowls. They must have been ones the family didn't use any more because they were dusty and grubby, like they'd been put away and left.

She closed the doors and opened the fridge, and even as it opened she caught the smell.

The fridge was full of food – plates and saucers covered in plastic film, fruit and meat still in its packing – but how long it had all been there, there was no saying. It was all of it rotten and mouldy.

It stank.

There were dead flies in a pool of water that had collected in the mush on the glass top of the salad box at the bottom.

She slammed the door and stepped back.

'You can look upstairs too,' said the girl.

Sophie turned round.

The girl and the boy had come quietly from the other room and were watching her from the open kitchen door. The boy ran back into the hall and did a slide on the floor.

'Other people who come usually look upstairs,' the girl said.

Behind her, the boy pressed the switch on the wall and the lights in the hall came on.

But Sophie was thinking about the fridge. It hadn't been emptied for ages – you couldn't live with a fridge like that.

She looked at the girl.

'Where have your mum and dad gone?' she said.

The girl didn't answer, she just stood there in her faded Minnie Mouse T-shirt.

'Look,' she said. 'I can open my mouth really wide.'

She opened it again for Sophie.

She managed a little bit more this time than she'd

done before, but it still wasn't really anything to make a fuss about.

'Yeah, you've shown me,' said Sophie.

The boy slid up on his socks beside the girl and pulled down his eyelid, but Sophie wasn't really in the mood for this any more. She was thinking about the fridge, and thinking that it might be better if she picked up her bag and went now.

But the girl and the boy just stood in the door.

'I can do it much more than that,' insisted the girl as though realising that Sophie hadn't been impressed with what she'd done. 'I can open it really wide.'

This time when she opened her mouth, she did it like she was yawning at the same time, and there was no mistaking that she could open her mouth really wide – Sophie could see her teeth and her tongue.

'Yeah, that's really quite wide,' said Sophie.

But now she just wanted to get her bag and go. She'd ring her mum when she got to the road – there'd be a signal there – and she'd tell her that there'd been no note and it was a really creepy house, and she wasn't going to do that one again.

The girl glanced at the boy, and they nodded at each other and smiled.

Then the girl looked at Sophie again.

'No,' she said. 'I can do it much wider than that.'

And there was something very horrible – spiteful, almost like a purr – in the way she said it.

She hunched her shoulders up to her ears and, dropping them sharply, tipped back her head and opened her mouth wide. Her teeth – all flat and white – parted her lips, and her mouth just kept getting wider and bigger. It didn't stop. Sophie couldn't see her T-shirt any more – the girl had become just one huge mouth. The bottom of it touched the floor and her tongue lolled out like a fat slab of wet fish. With a slurp she pulled it back in and the huge jaws slowly closed and shrank until the teeth were covered again by lips, and there was just the girl.

Sophie was shaking like a leaf, she couldn't utter a sound.

She pressed herself back against the cupboards. The girl wiped her mouth on the back of her hand, then the back of her hand on her Minnie Mouse T-shirt.

'I said I could,' she purred in that same horrible way.

The boy was standing next to the girl now. He was looking at Sophie too.

'And we can open our eye really wide.'

Sophie shook her head weakly and her voice was small, like a mouse – she didn't want to see.

'No.'

The boy put his fingers to below his eye, then he reached across until he was holding the skin with both hands and pulled it wider and wider. The skin stretched away until he held his arms wide. It was like looking into a dark sack. Sophie felt her breath stop in her chest.

There was something in the sack.

First one hand, and then another, gripped the lip of skin and, as steadily as if he were clambering over a low fence, a man made of strips of torn leather and dirty cotton stepped out of the boy's eye and into the room.

The boy let the skin of his eye close with a snap.

'Him and me,' said the boy. 'We're Tom.'

The leather-and-cotton man had a bent back and flattened nose. He grinned malevolently at Sophie. His teeth and eyes were white against his puckered, tanned face. He made to take a step forward, but the boy touched his sleeve and the man stopped. Sophie could see the man trembling to his very heels, every fibre of him wanting to be let go, like a dog on a leash.

'Now we can play chase,' said Tom. 'We'll chase . . .'

'. . . And I'll catch,' said Lucy. Her eyes were bright and sparkling, and she bit at the top of her lip as she said it. 'It's better if you hide though,' she said.

'Then we have to find you as well,' said Tom. 'And that makes chasing much more fun.'

'Let's count to fifty,' said Lucy.

'Sixty,' said Tom.

'No,' stammered Sophie.

'One,' said Tom. The leather-and-cotton man was staring at her with his white eyes and white teeth, he was quivering with excitement.

'You'll have to hide – quick,' said Lucy and clapped her hands.

'Two,' said Tom.

They didn't try to stop her. They just watched her run. Sophie went blindly down the hall, clattering to a stop against the front door, grabbing at the catch but the door wouldn't open. She twisted and pulled at it as hard as she could, but it wouldn't budge. Behind her, she could hear them counting. They were already at eighteen.

In utter panic she ran into the big front room and like a bird against the glass tried the window catches one by one – she could see the garden and the fish-pond and the sundial, but the windows wouldn't open, and the glass was so thick and heavy. It wouldn't break even when she hit it.

And they were still counting.

Through her panic a voice in her head – the only

quiet thing in her – remembered what the girl had said about the phone – about the signal.

They were still standing by the kitchen door. She fled past them and up the stairs onto the landing. There were stairs again after that and she took them two at a time. As she reached the top one she turned and listened – she could feel her heart thumping in her ears.

Downstairs, the counting had stopped.

The lights in the hall clicked out.

In the dim, almost dark, she heard a sound on the stairs below her, like the movement of leather and cotton.

Then she heard a whisper that carried in the dark: 'Let's look in the bathroom.'

It was the boy.

She saw the shape of him run, quick tippy-toes on socked feet, across the landing below her, then come back again.

'No, she's not in there.'

She could see the shape of the leather-and-cotton man too. She hadn't realised he was so close. He was standing on the turn of the stairs below her, halfway up, but he was looking the other way waiting, hand on the rail, for the boy.

'Let's look in the bedrooms,' said Tom.

He was almost squeaking with excitement now.

She saw him flit, tippy-toes, past again, and she saw the leather-and-cotton man go down. She pressed herself against the wall.

There was barely light for her to see anything beyond the landing she stood on. There were doors and another flight of stairs, she could see the dim shapes of those. Some of the doors were open. Barely breathing, she went as quietly as she could along the passage, peering into each open room she passed, but there was nowhere to hide in any of them – they were all empty. There wasn't even a cupboard. She pulled her phone out of her pocket, the screen lit up as she touched it. She clapped her hand quickly over it lest they see its light from below, then opened her fingers a crack and looked, but the little signal bar was empty.

She could hear the sound of the boy and the leather-and-cotton man searching through the rooms below her. They weren't even trying not to make any noise now.

She went up the last flight of stairs and found herself where the servants must have once lived – the passage was narrow and the floorboards bare. At the end of it, bolted to the wall like a fire escape, was a thin metal ladder with a hatch above it. She stood on the ladder and pushed at the hatch. It was only closed by a simple bolt. She slid the bolt and threw it open.

She could see the tiles of the roof and above them, the sky. She clambered up the ladder and out into the cold damp air. She was in a gully between sloping rooves with a low balustraded wall at the end of it, and nothing else beyond that but a straight drop to the garden below.

And she realised her mistake.

Through the hatch she could hear the sounds of feet on the bare floorboards inside. The sound of someone climbing the metal ladder. She looked down at the phone in her hand but even as she did, the head of the leather-and-cotton man poked through the hatch. He saw her and grinned – clambered up and onto the roof. The boy followed him.

'We found you!' he shouted.

Sophie backed away from them. The man, his arms spread wide, started slowly towards her. She could see the whites of his eyes and his grinning teeth. The balustrade wall caught her behind her knee and as she grabbed at it to steady herself, she felt her phone slip from her fingers.

She saw it slide across the top of the wall and drop.

'No!'

And she saw something else too.

At the bottom of the wall, as though she'd been standing there waiting all the time, was the girl in the Minnie Mouse T-shirt. Her face was turned up towards Sophie.

She saw Sophie and waved at her.

There was nowhere else for Sophie to go.

'Don't worry,' the girl called out, 'you can jump!'

And even in the dim light Sophie saw the girl's mouth beginning to part into a huge, cavernous smile – lips and teeth and tongue.

'I'll catch you,' said the girl.

This time, as the world became real again about him, the boy sat very still and said nothing. The air was cold and sharp now. He could see a sheen on the concrete of the platform, and he wasn't sure if it was frost or damp.

Next to him, the old man took out the packet of peppermints and popped another one into his mouth, offered one to the boy, but the boy shook his head.

'Not talking won't make any difference,' the man said quietly, as he put the packet back.

'To *what*?' said the boy.

The man looked at him, and the silence drew out – long, like a knife.

'To *how* quickly the time goes,' the man said, suddenly all brightness and smiles. 'Seems to go quicker though, if you're having a chat, doesn't it?

But it's always the same, doesn't go any quicker or slower. I mean, what's the time now?' He poked his finger at the boy. 'You should look on your phone thing. That'll tell you. Go on, you have a look on your phone.'

'No,' the boy said.

He almost said 'I can't' but he just stopped himself.

'Go on,' the man said encouragingly.

'No – if I don't look it will go quicker,' said the boy. 'Won't seem so long.'

'Be just the same,' the man answered. 'Just your perception of time, that's all that's different. You can watch those old hands round on the clock and some days they drag away the minutes, but if you're doing something busy – fwoo! They shoot by. They're always the same, though. Like I said . . .' His voice fell again. 'Won't make any difference.'

The boy heard the fall of the words and he looked uneasily down the platform to the dark end, willing the train to come.

'Rails will tell you when the train's coming,' the man said, as though he'd heard the thought. 'I've told you. You'll hear it before you see it.'

He rolled the mint around his mouth and it clicked against his teeth.

'Toby's got a clock,' he said.

For a moment, the boy thought the man meant a real clock – a watch – and he couldn't understand why a dog would have a watch.

The little dog turned its black shiny nose and bright eyes up to him.

'"Tummy time clock" I call it,' said the man. 'He sits by his bowl looking at me and, rain or shine, you can tell the time by Toby's tummy. I have to laugh when the clocks go back though, 'cause he's there an hour early, and I say, "You've got your tummy time clock wrong, Toby! It's not tummy time o'clock yet!"'

He laughed quietly to himself.

'Hmm, tummy time o'clock,' he said.

He turned and looked at the boy again.

'You at school?'

The boy nodded.

'You do exams and things like that?'

'Yeah.' He didn't want to talk any more.

'"Sit you down, get your pencil." That sort of thing?'

'Sort of.'

The man leaned towards him.

'What's the capital of Egypt?' he said.

The boy stared blankly at him and shook his head.

'I don't know.'

'Cairo,' the man said. 'What they teach you these days? Cairo. You should know that, that's where all the pyramids are.'

'We do other stuff these days,' the boy said.

'Well, that won't help you if you ever need to go to Cairo.'

'I don't want to go to Cairo,' he said, and he said it more sharply than he'd meant to. 'I just want the train to come.'

'Course you do,' said the man, soothingly. 'Train time o'clock, that's what you're wanting. That's what he's wanting, isn't it, Toby? Train time o'clock.'

The little dog looked up at its name and wagged its tail.

The man leaned towards the boy again.

'Oslo,' he said.

'I'm sorry?'

'That's the capital of Norway. Oslo.'

'I really don't think I care.'

'That's just geography,' the man said. 'There's worse things than geography. Worse things than that.'

And he began another story.

Picture Me

The funeral had been the week before. Sammie hadn't gone, but her mum and dad had. It was sad in the way that only unattended funerals can be, they'd said. Just the two of them and the old lady's coffin.

They'd had to collect the old lady's things from the Home too, but that was on another day, and Sammie's mum did it. By the time Sammie got in from school her mum was back. She'd already dropped a bag of the old lady's clothes off at a charity shop, but there'd been a photo album too, and her mum had kept that. It was on the side in the kitchen in a grey plastic bag.

'What relation was she?' asked Sammie.

She pulled the album out of the bag and turned it over in her hands. It had a worn, black leather cover and it smelled of stale perfume.

'Grandma's cousin,' her mum said. 'That's why I kept it – I thought there might be pictures of Grandma in there as a girl. It goes back years.'

'You never told me about her.'

Her mum shook her head.

'She lived most of her life in hospitals and homes of one sort or another – even from her teens. She wasn't quite right in the head, or something like that. Anyway, it was hers. I thought you'd be interested to see it. They said at the Home it upset her if they ever got it out – but they didn't want to throw it away. It

113

had just been left in a box. We don't have to keep it.'

'No, I'll look at it,' said Sammie.

She put the album back in the bag.

Her mum and dad were out that night – weren't going to be late, they said, back by ten-thirty. So after they'd gone, Sammie had a bath, then settled herself down at the big table in the kitchen with a cup of tea and got the album out again.

The smell was even stronger this time – of old cardboard and stale perfume, like it had been kept somewhere damp for years. She wasn't so sure she wanted to look at it any more. The smell got on her hands. It was so strong it almost made a noise in her head – a long discordant note – and she thought it was the fridge, but it was like it was the album and the smell doing it.

She turned a few pages with the tips of her fingers. It was just like any old album – baby pictures, christening, toddler, dressing up in the garden, days out, school – all neatly written up with where and when. 'Patricia's first birthday', 'Playing in the garden at Bridge Road'. Things like that. Sammie could see the girl growing up with each page she turned.

She was about to close it, had almost stopped paying any real attention to the pictures, when

114

something made her stop and look more carefully.

There'd been five or six pictures now of the old lady when she must have been about Sammie's own age, and Sammie couldn't understand why they were in the album at all. In each one the girl's face was turned towards the camera, and she looked so frightened. Her eyes were wide and her mouth parted as though she'd just drawn a breath, and there was no explanation for any of them – no writing underneath saying where they'd been taken or when, and Sammie wondered why would anyone want to keep those. Why keep a picture of a girl looking so frightened?

She flicked a few pages forward, and dotted through the album were more of the same. Only now they were pictures with nurses in and shared rooms like little wards. In each one the girl was the only person looking at the camera, and her face was so frightened. Sammie turned a whole load of pages, and there were more still – even when the girl was much older, even as an old lady in the Home. There she'd be, sitting in a lounge with other old people, balloons pinned up like it was someone's birthday, long tables with people sitting at them in Christmas paper hats. And her face was the only one in the whole room turned towards the camera – pale and gaunt and frightened.

Sammie looked up from the album. The kitchen

light was on, the rest of the house was dark and quiet. But she could still hear that noise, that long discordant note in her head. The heating must have gone off because the room was colder now than it had been. She could almost see her breath in the air. The house felt very empty and she felt alone. She looked at the clock on the cooker, hadn't noticed the time. Her mum and dad were already later than they'd said they'd be.

There were only two more pages of the album left to look at. Almost unwillingly now, she turned the first of them. There was a single picture. It was of the old lady. It was daylight and she was asleep in her bed – her head on the pillow, her eyes shut, her mouth just a little open.

Sammie turned the last page.

It took her a moment to understand what she was looking at, because it was a picture of her mum and dad, only not somewhere she recognised at all. But it had been taken recently, and she was trying to work out where it must have been. They were both wearing sombre clothes. Her dad was looking at a sheet of paper he was holding, and her mum was getting something out of her handbag. Neither of them was looking at the camera. Sammie didn't see the coffin at first, because it was in the background behind them and it looked just like a table, but it was there. It slowly dawned on her that it was the old lady's funeral – it had to be. That's what her mum and dad had been wearing, and that was the only time they had worn those clothes of late, and behind them was the coffin. She thought they'd said they'd been the only ones that went, but there must have been at least someone else to take the photo. Sammie turned the page back and looked again at the picture of the old lady asleep.

She was so still, so pale. Her lips deathly grey.

The phone rang.

The sound of it in the quiet, dark house made Sammie jump.

It was her dad. Someone's car had broken down and they were going to give the person a lift home. There was no point in Sammie staying up, he said. She tried to ask him about the photo at the funeral, but the line was bad, and he was already saying goodbye.

She put the phone down and went back to the kitchen, closed the album and slipped it into the plastic bag. She didn't want to look at it any more, those last pictures had unsettled her. As she went to bed she turned on the downstairs lights and left them on. It felt safer like that. Upstairs, in bed in the dark, she couldn't hear the noise in her head, but she could still smell the album, only it didn't smell like perfume now – it smelled like stale, cheap aftershave. She got up and went to the bathroom and washed her hands clean, but she could still smell it.

In the morning she tried to explain to her mum about the pictures, but they were late already and her mum didn't really listen – just said the old lady hadn't been right in her head, and that probably explained it.

All day, Sammie kept thinking about those pictures of the old lady. They'd really disturbed her. She didn't know why the girl had looked so frightened or why the pictures were even in the book. Was that what her mum had meant about not being right in the head – is that what being ill in your head looked like?

It made her shiver.

She could still smell the album too – the smell of stale aftershave. Sometimes she couldn't tell if it was just in the back of her nose or if someone was actually wearing it, and she'd find herself looking round trying to work out who it was. She'd say to her friends, 'Can't you smell that?' But none of them could smell it.

At the end of the day she had to go back into school to get a top she'd forgotten from the empty changing rooms. She had to hunt around under the metal lockers until she found it, and that wasn't nice because she was all alone and she could smell after-shave again. There were little clicks and noises like there was someone else there, and that spooked her, so that she called out, but the place was empty.

She was glad to get home. It had been a horrible day.

There was work she had to do in the evening, but she didn't feel like doing it at all. She lay on the sofa in her comfy socks going through messages and pictures on her phone while her mum cooked dinner. She was looking at pictures of last summer mostly. She liked them. It was just like the old lady's album if she thought about it – days out, the river, the cathedral green. She swiped through the pictures. She'd taken some at school in the morning. It made her smile when she found them because there were a couple she hadn't taken. Her friends would do that sometimes – pinch someone else's phone when they weren't looking, take dumb pictures and put it back before the person realised it had gone. There was one of her on the walkway between lessons, and another one in class. She couldn't work out who had taken them, and it made her smile.

The very last one was of her looking for her top under the lockers in the changing rooms, and who-ever had taken that must really have sneaked up because they'd been standing right behind her. She grinned when she saw it because she'd known there was someone there.

But then her face clouded in a frown.

She'd had her phone then, she was sure of it.

She looked more carefully at the detail in the picture – and yes, she could see the phone, it was on the bench by her hand – so that didn't make any sense.

She couldn't work out how it could have been done. She sent a couple of messages to her friends, but no one would admit they'd done it, and then it wasn't funny any more, it was just plain creepy because that wasn't a nice trick to play on anyone.

She was still cross about it when she went to bed. She could still smell that aftershave too. She washed her hands and face twice trying to get rid of it.

She'd been asleep for a while when something woke her. She didn't know what it was. Everything was dark and quiet, and the bed was warm.

She lay very still, listening.

There wasn't a sound, and though she knew it was a stupid thing and that she was safe in her own bed in her own home, she suddenly just didn't feel safe at all. She reached out into the dark and turned on the bedside light, but there was nothing there – just her things across the floor where she'd dropped them; her posters on the wall, the chest of drawers. For all that though, that feeling of unease just didn't go away. She sat herself up in bed with the light on and looked around. Her eyes kept being drawn to one corner of the room, but there was nothing there. She could hear her mum and dad stirring in their room, but then everything was quiet again. After a while she got up and went down the hall to the bathroom. She could almost have believed that someone was following her and she stopped and looked behind, but there was only the dark hall and the spill of light from her door.

The bulb in the bathroom had gone that evening and they didn't have another one, so Sammie sat on the loo in the dark. When she was done she poured herself a glass of water from the sink. There was just enough moonlight through the window for her to see her own grey, grainy reflection in the big mirror. The feeling of unease still hadn't left her. She could see herself and the empty room – but she could still smell stale, cheap aftershave. She put her fingers to her nose, it wasn't on her hands.

She shook the last drops of water from the glass and put it upside down on the shelf, then went back down the hall to her room. But it still didn't feel right. She got into bed and sent a few messages on her phone, but no one else was awake and that only made things feel worse – made her feel more alone. She didn't know when it was she finally fell asleep, but her light was still on in the morning when her mum came in with a mug of tea and shook her awake.

She was so tired.

She propped herself up on her pillow, drank the tea and read the answers to the messages she'd sent in the night – but no one had said anything about the changing room. She opened her photos to look at that picture again, to see if she could work out how it had been done and who'd done it. She swiped through the day before – the walkway, the class-room, the changing room . . . and then she stopped, because there was another picture – a new one.

She couldn't believe what she was looking at. The mug of tea slipped through her fingers, spilled all over her duvet – soaked straight through – but she didn't even notice. That picture was all she could see.

It was of her, in the night.

She was holding a glass of water, standing in front of the mirror in the dark bathroom in her big, bed-time T-shirt – the one she was still wearing. The picture was of her reflection. She could see the out-line of the empty bath behind her, and the towels and the wall, and there was a man with a camera standing against the wall. He was all grainy and grey in the dark and had the camera up to his eye, so she couldn't see his face, just the impression of his jacket in the dark – it was one of those 1950s blazers old men wear with an embroidered badge on the pocket, like they've been in the army.

Her mum heard her shriek. She came up the stairs and Sammie was beside herself, but her mum couldn't get a word of sense out of her. Just something about a photo on her phone – only Sammie had dropped the phone and they couldn't find it in the bed, and when they did, it wouldn't switch on, and when it did switch on—

there weren't any pictures on it.

None like she'd said.

No walkway, no classroom, no changing room, no bathroom.

None of them.

It wasn't that her mum didn't believe her, but how can you believe something that isn't there?

'You had a dream, Sammie. You had a broken night.'

That's what her mum said.

There was no telling her otherwise. Sammie tried, but her mum just got more short with her. In the end her mum told her to stop it, get herself sorted and go to school – like she used to when Sammie was pretending she had a cold – and there was nothing else Sammie could do.

But when she sat on the bus, opened her phone and looked again, the pictures were there. None of her friends caught that bus, and she didn't know what to do. She could smell stale aftershave, like someone was wearing it on the seat behind her, and she turned and looked, but the seat was empty and the rest of the bus was just the people she saw every day.

All her teachers said that she didn't look well. They asked if something was wrong at home – they had to do that nowadays – but how could she explain? She tried. She told the people who mattered, and they said 'show us' and when she showed them, there weren't any pictures on her phone. They were only there when she looked at it alone.

On the bus home there were two new pictures. One was of Sammie in the queue in the school cafe. She was reaching forward for an apple – she remembered she hadn't wanted to eat anything, and when she got it, the apple had tasted like the smell of stale after-shave, so she'd thrown it away.

But the second picture, that made no sense at all.

It had been taken inside the supermarket in town. It took her a moment to work out whereabouts in the shop it was, but she got it – it was on the aisle where the biscuits were stacked. A group of people were standing looking at something on the ground. Sammie was the only one who was looking at the camera. She'd been caught in the moment of turning round, her face was so frightened – eyes wide, mouth open – just like the old lady in the album.

She could hear that sound in her head again as she looked at the picture.

Only nothing like this had ever happened. Sammie hadn't been in the supermarket for at least a week and she'd have remembered this. She stared at the photo.

She wanted to show her mum the pictures of the old lady in the album when she got home, but when she tried, they couldn't find the album. It wasn't until it was dark and Sammie went to bed that she found it. It was poked under her clothes on the floor, and all the clothes smelled of stale, cheap aftershave like someone had touched them.

She had another broken night.

There was no new photo the next morning.

Nor the morning after that.

But Sammie knew it would happen again. She just knew it. She felt crawling-sick inside all the time.

She wouldn't go into the bathroom on her own either. Her mum had to stand by the open door. Her mum didn't want to. When her dad came home from work, she heard her mum whispering to him about it in the kitchen, but she stopped when Sammie came in.

Later in the evening her dad gave her a big hug and wanted to know if everything was all right at school, and she tried to tell him too, but there were no photos on her phone when she did, and she saw the look he gave her mum.

She couldn't sleep that night. She sat up with her light on – she looked like a ghost by the morning. Pale and frightened.

But her mum said she had to go to school. So she did.

She wouldn't have gone to the supermarket though, but when she got to the bus station her friend, Mill, was waiting for her and she wanted to get something for lunch. Mill just dragged Sammie with her. She wouldn't let her say no.

The strip lights in the store were hard and bright, and the tills were morning empty. Mill got her drink, got some rolls, and then she said she wanted some biscuits from the biscuit aisle. They came round the corner and there was a group of people standing with their backs to them.

An old man was on the ground – his glasses had come off and he'd dropped all his shopping, it was all over the floor – the store first-aider was holding his hand.

And Sammie felt the world stop.

She turned quickly round to look behind her – eyes wide, mouth open – knowing that this was the moment the picture of her was taken—

only there was no one there to take it. The aisle was empty.

She tried to show Mill the picture of the supermarket on her phone, show her the others too, but there were no pictures there – none of them – and the more she tried, the less Mill believed her. Mill just laughed and said Sammie was 'being weird' and then Sammie cried and cried.

Mill put her arm round her and walked her into school, still crying.

The school couldn't get hold of her mum straight away, so Sammie sat in the first-aid room until they did. But the whole time she knew there was someone there watching her. She could feel it. She asked the first-aider to look at her phone, but there were no pictures on it, and then Sammie didn't know if they'd even been there at all, and she cried again.

Finally, they got hold of her mum. She came and took Sammie home. She said they'd get her an appointment with the doctor in the afternoon, but they couldn't get one until the next day, so Sammie lay on the sofa with her duvet over her while her mum did things round the house. She didn't want to be upstairs on her own. Her phone kept pinging, and she knew it was people at school, messaging to see if she was all right, but she didn't want to answer. Didn't want to touch her phone.

But she couldn't help wanting to know if there was another picture. If there wasn't, then maybe she had imagined it all, and everything would be all right. That's why she looked.

Her mum had put the phone on the side out of harm's way. It had caused enough trouble already, she'd said. So Sammie waited until her mum had gone upstairs. She crept off the sofa and took it from the side.

The phone smelled of stale, cheap aftershave. It was warm to the touch, as though someone had just been holding it the moment before, or it had been in their pocket.

She opened the photos.

They were all there, every one of them – changing room, bathroom, cafe, supermarket – and there was a new one too.

In that picture, Sammie was wearing the cardigan her mum had given her for her last birthday, only it was all stretched now, and she was wearing it half on her shoulders and half off, as though she didn't care. She was sitting in a large airy room that she knew she'd never been in. A woman in a blue uniform and slacks was pushing a tea tray full of cups and saucers towards the door behind her, and there were balloons pinned up and long tables with people sitting at them in Christmas paper hats. Sammie's face was gaunt and pale and frightened. She looked so lost.

She was the only person in the whole room looking at the camera.

The man didn't look at the boy. He just held the lead and tapped his shoes on the platform.

The boy got up and walked away, right down to the end where the platform sloped into darkness. He wanted to be on his own, as far away from the man as he could get, but he felt as though someone had walked down there in the darkness with him, only that was stupid because it was just the story, and it was far better to be standing there than sitting next to that old man.

The air smelled cold and clean, not of anything perfumed, but he shivered nonetheless.

Looking back along the platform, he could see the three pools of light cast by the lamps on the poles, and the bench with the old man and the lantern on the ground between his feet.

He was just sitting there.

The boy wondered how long it would be before the train came, tried listening for the sound in the rails, but there was nothing. He started to count – give it twenty and the train would come.

Give it sixty.

One hundred.

Only there was no train, just the damp, cold dark and a silence that was thick and heavy as velvet.

He didn't know what the real time was, he'd lost all sense of that, but it seemed like an age, and there was no way of him knowing. Maybe the old man had a watch – maybe he could sneak a look at it on his wrist if he went back and sat next to him, but he didn't want to go back, and he didn't want to sit next to him.

He made himself count to one hundred.

One hundred and sixty.

But there was no train.

The man was still sitting on the bench, and that at least made the boy feel better. He could just stand here until the train came, only it was dark and he wished he could stop thinking about those stories, because it was as though each one of them had happened right in front of him, and whenever he looked out into the flat empty darkness he saw them like shapes, heard them like whispers.

He looked at his phone again, but it didn't work.

He thought of his dad and his mum and how worried they'd be.

It was only then he realised that the little dog was standing next to him, its lead lying on the cold ground. He hadn't heard it coming, didn't know how long it had been there. It turned its scruffy little head up towards him and wagged its tail. He looked from it, back down the platform to the man and the lantern. The man was still sitting on the bench. He hadn't moved at all.

Wasn't moving at all. Was quite motionless.

'Oh, no,' the boy whispered.

He picked up the lead and hesitantly, almost holding his breath, started to walk back. The dog trotted along next to him. It stopped to sniff at the concrete wall.

'No, come on,' he said and tugged at the lead.

The man was unnaturally still, almost slumped on the bench. As the boy got closer he could see his hands in his lap. His eyes were open, but he didn't turn to look at him – he just stared blankly ahead.

His skin was sallow in the pale light. In those last couple of steps the boy could see the frayed collar and not quite straight tie. See the white tufts of bristle on the man's chin where he'd missed them shaving, like old men do. But the man didn't move.

The boy stood looking at him, not knowing what to do.

Then, suddenly, the man turned his head and looked straight at him.

'You had a little walk then?' he said cheerfully.

The boy gave a start and stepped back.

'Oh, you brought Toby back – you needn't have minded. He goes wandering off. Never goes far though.'

'I thought you were—'

'Dead?' the man said.

'You done that on purpose, didn't you?' said the boy. 'Is that your "game" – make me think you're dead, scare the life out of me? Well it's not bloody funny!'

'Language.'

'And you can have your bloody dog back!'

He threw the lead at the man.

Unperturbed, the man bent forward and picked it up.

'What made you think I was dead, son?' he said.

'You weren't moving.'

'I was just sitting still! Person can sit still, can't they? I was just sitting, thinking about that brother of yours.'

The boy could see the man's eyes again now – watery eyes, that somehow didn't seem to fit in that

133

face. They were hard, like shards of dark glass, and the boy didn't want him to be thinking about his brother. Didn't like the thought of that at all.

'Old is it, your house?' the man said. ''Cause I've got a story about a little boy and an old house.'

'I don't want to hear it!'

'Well I've got to tell it, haven't I? Can't not tell it if we're to play my game.'

Soot

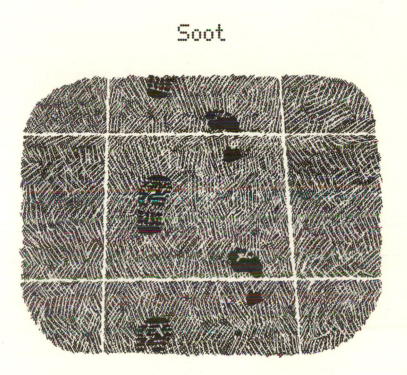

It was an old house – new to them, but an old house all the same. It hadn't been a month since they'd moved in, and they hadn't got used to the noises it made yet – the way it settled and creaked at night, or the way the water pipes knocked whenever a tap was turned on. There was nothing scary in them though, nothing harmful. It was a bit of a joke, really.

And now Sara stood with her ear pressed against her little brother's bedroom wall. He had his ear pressed to the wall as well. He'd found a new noise.

'Can you hear that?' he said.

She listened carefully.

'That!' he said again.

Her eyes widened, and he could see that she'd heard it.

'It's not the noise the pipes make,' he said. 'They go "lumpa-lumpa-lumpa-lumpa".'

He was only five – younger by ten years than she was. His name was Chris.

She stood back and looked at the wall, followed the line of it to the shelved alcoves on either side. The wall was covered in faded paper, all stripes and flowers and stained with the passage of years. The paper was going to come off soon enough and be covered instead with rockets and superheroes.

'I think this was a chimney,' she said. 'There'd

have been a fireplace here once.' She looked down at Chris. 'Maybe it's a bird's nest?'

They put their ears to the wall and listened again. As if in answer to their curiosity – as if whatever had been making the sound had been waiting for them to come back – it started again.

Tap.

Tap, tap.

'Or rats?' She pulled a face. Neither of them liked the thought of rats very much, so she went and fetched their dad.

They stood, all three of them, listening at the wall. Then they went down the stairs and out into the summer garden and looked up at the clear blue sky and the line of tall chimney pots that divided their roof from the house next door. Their little dog sat by them and looked too.

'There's probably a nest at the top,' said their dad. 'A chick's fallen out of it.'

'How will it get back up?' asked Sara.

Her dad shook his head.

'I'm not sure it will, honey,' he said.

They stood staring at the roof and the line of pots.

'In the old days they used to send little boys up to clean chimneys like that,' he said. 'They got stuck sometimes.'

He put his hand on Chris's head.

'Fancy going up, Chrissy? Put you in at the bottom, pull you out at the top?'

Chris pushed his dad's hand away, and looked at the chimney again.

'It's not fair,' he said. 'I want it to get out.'

The little bird in the chimney clouded the day for them. They knew that when they couldn't hear it scratching any more, it would be because it had died – all alone in the tight, narrow dark. Chris kept going back into his room just to check on it, to make sure it was still alive. He whispered little words of encouragement to it through the wall.

They could still hear it when Chris went to bed – the noise of it kept him awake. In the middle of the night he came into Sara's room and woke her up, led her down the hall to his door. She could hear it still, tapping from inside the chimney. Louder than before.

It was still there when they put their ears to the wall in the morning.

The thought of just leaving it to die in the dark chimney became intolerable. Their dad said if it had lasted the whole night, then it deserved its chance – and they were going to decorate the room anyway, so what would it matter if they made a mess now?

They cleared Chris's things away and, putting down an old decorating sheet, they began peeling the paper off the wall. It came away like dry, dusty lengths of old skin – layer on layer of it. The very last of it was stuck onto Victorian newspapers that had been used as lining. The newspapers came away too. Sara sat on the floor and read the scraps of print.

When she looked up again, her dad had got right down to the bare plaster.

Sara could see now where the old fireplace had been bricked in. But above that, higher up the chimney breast, another hole had been filled in too – as if someone had needed to get at something there once before, and had plastered over it when they were done.

'If we get the bird out, can we keep it?' said Chris.

'If it's small, we'll look after it,' said their dad, 'but when it's ready, we'll let it go. Understand?'

Chris nodded.

Their dad took a hammer and a small chisel, and started chipping away the plaster, then raked out the mortar between the bricks. He chose the higher of the two holes, because when he'd stood on a chair and listened at the wall, it sounded like the tapping was coming from there rather than the closed-up fireplace below. He stopped every now and then, and they took it in turns to get onto the chair and listen to the bird. But the sounds it made were becoming painful to hear.

'We're scaring it,' said Chris, and he put his hands over his ears to block the noise out.

As their dad loosened the last of the bricks, the noises became more desperate – as though something was beating its life out against the other side of the wall – right up to the moment before the hole through was finally made. As the soot of years cascaded out of it like a dirty river of muck and twigs, spilling in a rush onto the sheet on the floor, and filling the air with acrid black dust, the noise simply stopped. When everything had settled there was only a breath of chill air from the hole – far colder than the day outside.

A breath of chill air, and absolute silence.

Their dad peered in – looked up, looked down.

'It's gone,' he said. 'Must have just needed the noise we made to get it going.'

He shone a torch in just to be certain it had gone, but there was nothing there. Then they saw him reach in and bring something down, only it wasn't a bird he held in his hand.

It was a small leather boot.

The leather was biscuit dry, scuffed and stained with rain and soot. It still had the laces in. He climbed down off the chair and they all looked at it. It was about the size of Chris's foot – they measured the two of them together and they were the same.

'It was probably in there for luck,' said their dad. 'You find things in old chimneys.'

But something about that just didn't seem right to Sara. It was something about the silence and the cold air – there was nothing lucky about that. She looked up at the ragged hole. It was nearer the ceiling than the floor.

'Even up there? How would they get it right up there?'

But her dad was pulling the edges of the decorating sheet together and making a pile of the dirt and soot. He wasn't listening. There was dirt and soot everywhere – on their faces, in their hair, down their necks. It covered everything. They could even taste it, like grit between their teeth. It tasted bitter, like the smell of the chimney.

As it was a hot day, Sara put up the orange paddling pool in the garden and filled it with warm water. While their dad was sorting out the mess in the room she washed Chris in it – put the watering can, and then the hose on him – made rainbows with her finger over the end. They tried to get the dog in as well – that was always a good game, 'soak the dog' they called it – but he wouldn't come near them and that was odd. He slunk away. Even when Sara picked him up and tried to put him in with Chris, he twisted wildly in her arms and bit her so that she dropped him. He'd never done that before. He wouldn't come back to her either.

She ran her hand under the tap in the kitchen, then went upstairs and had a shower. As she dried her hair she looked down from the window onto the garden. Chris was still in the paddling pool, but he was playing pretend now – she could see him talking to someone who wasn't there, tipping the watering can high over their head as well as his own.

She put a plaster on her hand and went back down to the garden, told him to get out of the paddling pool while she tipped the dirty water away. She filled it with clean water, but it didn't seem to matter how often she changed it, the water ended up just as full of soot. She couldn't work out where it was all coming from. Chris didn't make it easy for her either. He ran in and out of the water the whole time like a wild thing – showing off just like he did when he had a friend round to play. She didn't like him very much when he was like that, and he was like it all day. He ran in and out of the house so often. There were lines of wet footprints up the path and across the tiles of the kitchen floor. She could see where he'd only bothered to put one of his trainers on because she could make out the two lines of wet footprints – one foot bare, one foot shod. She gave up even trying to mop them up. At the end of the day when he came in at last, she put a cloth over them all and the cloth came away dark with soot.

In fact, she couldn't get any real sense out of him all day. He took himself into corners and carried on his pretend game there, talking to himself. Whenever she came too close, he'd stop and wait until she'd gone before he'd start it again, and she'd hear him giggle as she walked off, as though he was laughing at her with someone else. Even when he came in, he was like it.

Their dad had tidied Chris's bedroom – stacked the bricks back into the hole in the chimney. He said he'd put some mortar in them when he could, but Chris didn't seem to mind. Long after they'd put him to bed they could still hear him jumping around in his room. He made so much noise that Sara went up to tell him to quieten down. She found him breathless and red-faced. All the thumping had loosened even more soot from the chimney. It was on the carpet and over his bed. There were dirty handprints of it on the white of his pillow.

And there was something else wrong too, not just with Chris. They couldn't get the dog to come back into the house at the end of the day, he just wouldn't do it. As it was warm they put his basket and water bowl by the back door and left him in the garden with the porch light on. But when Sara looked out of the window as she went to bed, she couldn't see him anywhere.

Long into the night, she was woken up by the sound of Chris still playing – he was talking to himself too, and that was really annoying. She could hear him through the wall. She pulled the bedclothes over her head, but at last it was too much for her to get any sleep, and she got up and went in to him. He was running about, his toys spread all over the floor. He'd managed to get soot on them too, and his pyjamas.

'You need to get to sleep,' she said, and she put him in his bed, but he looked up at her, all excitable and grinning, so pleased with himself, and the moment she was out of the door she heard him get out of bed, laughing and giggling.

'Shut up!' she snapped, and closed the door behind her.

In the morning, they couldn't find the dog at all. There was no sign of him, and that was a worry. He hadn't learned this house yet – not like the old one – and it backed onto open fields. There was a wall and a small fence, but if he'd got through that, he could be anywhere, and beyond the fields was an old quarry – it was like half a hillside with a dead drop, straight down.

And if that wasn't bad enough, there was Chris.

Sara and Dad just didn't know what had got into him, but he must have been awake the whole night. They found him sitting on the floor of his room – it was a complete mess. Everything that could be pulled out and played with, had been pulled out and left over the floor. He was red-eyed, almost weeping with exhaustion, and his face was so pale. When they asked him what on earth was the matter, he just wouldn't tell them. But he looked so frightened. He bit his lip and shook his head, like it was a secret that wasn't to be told. He'd got soot everywhere. When Sara helped him out of his pyjama top, he'd got it up his arms too, like big pinch marks on his skin. He wouldn't eat any breakfast either, but when they were clearing up afterwards, they found him trying to take food from the kitchen and hide it in his room.

It didn't make any sense.

When Sara went into her own room, she found he'd been in there too – in her drawer. There were sooty finger marks over all her things. He had no business to be there. There were finger marks on the towels in the bathroom as well. There was soot, and the smell of the chimney, everywhere.

But for the moment, she was more bothered about the dog.

She said she'd take Chris with her and go looking

for it – thought that doing that might calm him down. Their dad told her that if they were going to go across the fields she had to be careful of the quarry, and she wasn't to let Chris go anywhere near the edge. She took the lead and they tried the streets in front of the house first – but no one had seen the dog. Chris hardly said a word the whole time, and when he did it was only to mumble. Sara had to put her ear close to even hear him. But he walked right next to her and held onto her so tightly, and he hardly ever did that. A couple of times it felt to her like he was actually trying to hide behind her, but when she bent down and looked into his face and asked him, 'What's wrong, Chrissy?', he just went very quiet, and wouldn't look at her.

At last, there was nowhere else to search for the dog but across the fields at the back. The grass was waist high there, and Sara stood in the middle of it – the lead in her hand – shouting the little dog's name over and over again. But he didn't come, and when she stopped and listened all she could hear was the sound of the grass moving in the warm breeze. Chris stood silent as a ghost next to her.

They were getting closer to the quarry now – a couple of ruined sheds stood at the edge of the field. Neither had a roof or a door, and she looked in them, but there was no sign of the dog. Chris followed her

147

all the time, never more than inches away. He stood by the doorway when she went in, but his eyes were always on the field outside. Then all of a sudden he caught hold of her hand.

'Make him go away,' he whispered. 'I don't want to play with him any more. Make him go away!'

'Who go away?' she said.

'Him,' he whispered.

She looked out through the door.

'There's nobody there, Chris.'

She bent down to him.

'Is someone at school bothering you?'

His face creased into tears, then he went quite rigid, absolutely white, his eyes fixed on the empty doorway behind her. No matter how much she tried to soothe him, he wouldn't say a word.

'You've still got soot on you,' she said gently.

He had a little smudge of it down his cheek that she hadn't noticed until then. She licked her finger and wiped it off. She meant it kindly, but it only made him cry even more. Then, over his shoulder through the open doorway, she saw the dog in the long grass.

'It's Barney!' she said.

She took off, shouting the dog's name. She saw it turn and look at her. It hesitated, as though torn between obedience and fear, then it bolted back into the long grass. By the time she'd given up chasing it, she was almost across the other side of the field. Hot and breathless, she looked back at the ruined sheds. From where she was now, she saw with alarm just how close they were to the twisted wire fence and the quarry drop, and she couldn't see Chris any more.

As she started back towards the sheds she heard a cry, and her stomach tightened.

'Chris!'

She broke into a run, stumbling on the uneven ground and almost falling into the doorway where she'd left him, but he wasn't there. Beside herself, she ran out and along the edge of the wire fence, looking down the dead drop into the crevices and the rocks and brambles below.

'Chris! Chris!'

Then, from behind her, she heard him laughing. She turned and saw him climbing back from underneath the wire. He was laughing at her like it was the best joke ever.

She was so angry.

'Don't ever do that again!' she shouted and she shook him hard.

But he just laughed more.

She caught hold of his wrist and jerked him back towards the house, and then she saw that he must have hit his head on something – on a rock or a stone – because there was a big bruise and it was bleeding, and all her anger just evaporated in that single moment.

'What have you done, Chrissy?'

He just laughed at her again. He pulled himself away from her hands and ran circles through the long grass until he fell down breathless on his back. He couldn't have been more different from how he'd been earlier. She was really worried then, that he must have hurt himself – he wouldn't even talk right either, he put on a silly, squeaky little voice.

'Talk properly, Chris,' she said.

But he just laughed and ran away again.

Eventually she got him back to the house and he sat quietly enough while their dad looked at his head. Chris didn't say anything at all as the bruise and cut were washed clean, he just held onto their dad's hand and smiled at him, and their dad ruffled his hair and said he was a real tough nut.

But her dad was furious with her – said anything could have happened, said that he'd told her to take care and this is what she'd done. And he was right, he had told her, but it all seemed so unfair because it was Chris who'd climbed under the wire. It was his stupid joke that had got him hurt.

Their dad put Chris on the sofa with a blanket

over him, then sat with his arm round him and read to him from one of the picture books he had had for his birthday. There didn't seem that much wrong with him now, and though her dad never saw him do it, every time Chris caught Sara's eye he'd smirk at her. It was really unpleasant, and so unlike him, but she couldn't say anything about it because it had been her fault he'd got hurt in the first place, and her dad had already had a go at her once.

So she went back out into the field to look for the dog – took his empty dinner bowl and rattled dry biscuits in it, but if he heard it, he didn't come. She left the bowl by the back door just in case.

Their dad was on shifts. By the time she'd got back from the field, he had already changed into his work clothes. He'd left Chris on the sofa with the blanket and his books. He gave her a hug and a kiss, and then he was gone.

When the door closed behind him, the house felt so empty. Not like it normally did. It wasn't just the dog not being there, it was something else – something that felt wrong in the house – and she couldn't say what that was. It might have been to do with the hole in the chimney, because the house felt cold and it smelled of soot.

Her dad had left the cloth and the bowl of water he'd used to clean up Chris on the draining board.

She tipped the water into the sink and there was even soot in that.

She got on and made some lunch. They sat at the kitchen table and ate it, but Chris shoved the food into his mouth with both hands like a little animal. He looked up and stopped mid-movement when he realised she was staring at him. His eyes not leaving her, he slowly picked up the fork and used that, but he did it as though he wasn't sure how to.

Then he grinned at her – a big white-toothed grin.

'Don't do that, Chris,' she said.

But he only grinned even more, and she wanted her dad to come back home because she didn't like being on her own looking after him, not like this.

It was as though he was playing a game with her.

He followed her around all day, but he never said anything. She'd look up and find him watching her – standing at her bedroom door looking in at her. She tried to ignore him, to pretend he wasn't there, but that made no difference. And when she got angry with him, he just laughed at her. It didn't matter what she said or did. There was nowhere in the house that he didn't follow her. Even if she closed a door, she could hear him standing outside it, waiting.

She tried to ring her dad at work on his mobile, but he didn't pick up.

There was nothing for her to do but watch the

clock round until she could get Chris into bed, and then her dad could sort it all out in the morning.

He didn't want to go to bed though, and she didn't know what to do. But he stayed upstairs and that was something. Finally she couldn't hear him moving round and she went quietly up to his room so as not to wake him. But he wasn't asleep.

He was lying on the bed in his pyjamas and he grinned at her when she came in. She looked at all the toys strewn across the floor.

'You go to sleep now, Chris,' she said.

She tucked his duvet round him, and as she looked into his face, it was almost as though it wasn't him, as though another boy was looking at her out of his eyes.

As she bent over him he reached up and, putting his arms round her neck, he kissed her hard on her mouth. She pulled herself away, wiping her lips and looking at him, angry and offended, but he only grinned at her.

His kiss had tasted acrid and bitter.

She stood wiping her mouth with the back of her hand. As she did she could see the reflection of her face in the mirror beside his bed—

and her lips were smudged with soot.

'I'm not listening,' the boy said. 'I'm not listening any more. Not to you, not to your stupid stories.'

He hadn't meant to listen to that one either, had tried not to, but it had just rolled over him, fixed him to the spot, and he'd been standing in the garden, feeling the warmth of the sunny day, the breeze, hearing the whisper of the long grass in the field behind the house. He could taste the bitterness of the kiss in his mouth.

He turned his back on the man and walked deliberately away along the platform. This time he'd stay there at the end of it, come what may – he'd just wait for the train. That's all he had to do – wait for the train. The man didn't matter, he didn't have to talk to him.

There was a frost now. The boy could see it for sure, sparkling on the concrete in the white-yellow of the station lamps. He stood in the last cone of light looking at it. Only once did he glance back down the platform to the bench. The man was feeding the little dog another biscuit, but, as though he'd felt the boy's glance, he turned and looked straight back at him.

The man was like that, turned and looking towards the boy, when without so much as a warning, not so much as even a flicker, the station lamps went out.

Pik.

For a moment there was a tiny, diminishing glow inside their glass covers, and then nothing, just darkness. The boy couldn't even see the edge of the platform. The only light that was left was the lantern on the ground between the old man's feet. The man was lit by it, still turned and looking at the boy – like a small painted picture surrounded by darkness. Then the man turned away.

The boy could feel his resolve to stay there and stand in the dark at the end of the platform slipping from him. There was nothing he could do to stop it. The more he fought to hold onto it, the more it ebbed, and the more he could believe that, quietly and slowly, something wicked was creeping through the darkness towards him, getting closer every moment he delayed.

He moved a few steps nearer to the light of the lantern, trying at the same time to be further from the dark, but no nearer to the man, only the spill of that light seemed to shrink the closer he came to it, as though it were drawing him in until finally he was standing again by the end of the bench and the old man.

'I said they'd turn those lights out,' the man chirruped. 'Saves a bit of money. No point having lights on if there's no one to see them. Be different if there was anyone to see them.' He leaned forward on the bench and looked exaggeratedly both ways into the darkness of the platform as if he might just see someone they hadn't noticed. 'No,' he said brightly. 'Just you and me and Toby.'

He smiled up at the boy.

'Just you and me,' he said quietly, and smiled again.

The boy didn't like that smile.

'You need to come and sit down,' the man said. 'No point standing over there in the cold on your own.'

'I'm happy here,' the boy answered.

'Suit yourself.'

'I will.'

'Nowhere else to go now though, is there?' said the man. 'You're going to have to stay with Toby and me unless you want to wander off and stand all alone in the dark.'

The boy didn't answer.

The old man tapped his feet on the cold platform, one then the other – tap tap tappity tap.

'Nearly time,' he said, but he didn't say what for.

The boy looked back into the darkness of the platform, that sense of there being something wicked, there in the dark, hadn't left him.

'What it is,' said the old man, shifting on the bench, 'is you've got to tell me a story. That's what's got to happen now. Anything you like – little story about your school, or what you did in the holidays. That's all you've got to do – tell me about your school. I'd like to hear about that. Then we can play my game.'

'I don't want to tell you a story.'

'Well we can't just wait here without a bit of a chinwag,' the man said. 'Tell a story and the time will see to itself – that train will be here and you'll be on it and on your way.'

The boy said nothing.

The man looked at him with those hard, shard-glass eyes.

'All right,' he said. 'Then I'll tell you another one.'

Dead Molly

There were only two more weeks of school left before the summer. Exams had finished and there was hardly any point in being there because no one was doing anything. Even the staff were counting down the days. It was so hot too, the sky so blue, so clear – boys with their sleeves rolled up, girls barefoot on the playing field, carrying their shoes on the tips of their fingers.

It was lunch break.

Richard and the others lay on their backs in the long grass at the edge of the playing field. Next year someone would have passed their test by now, and they'd have a car and could go somewhere, but not yet.

Richard rolled over onto his elbows. It was too hot to do anything.

'Let's play Dead Molly,' he said.

They used to play it all the time when they were little – it was such a good game. They'd choose who was going to be Molly, then lie on their backs with their eyes screwed shut and all say the rhyme together.

'One, two, she's coming for you,
Three, four, knocks at the door,
Dead Molly, poison my cup,
Dead Molly, wake me up!'

Then they'd open their eyes at exactly the same time, only whoever was Molly would have crept soundlessly up and stuffed their face inches away from someone else's, so when that person opened their eyes they'd find a face right against theirs.

'Boo!'

It would scare the daylights out of them – you never knew if it would be you. If you were Molly you had to be dead quiet so you wouldn't be heard – and you had to stop breathing as well, so the other person wouldn't feel any breath on their face. If you had long hair you had to hold that out of the way too – even a strand of it would give you away.

There was supposed to have been a Molly once, but nobody believed it. When Richard was small he'd told his gran he'd played Dead Molly at school, and she'd said he shouldn't mess with things like that, or one day he might get more than he'd bargained for. But it was just a game.

Because it was his idea, Richard was Molly first. He chose Ginny to scare, because it would be nice putting his face close to hers. He held his breath and silently leaned over her while they chanted the rhyme.

'One, two, she's coming for you,
Three, four, knocks at the door,

162

Dead Molly, poison my cup,
Dead Molly, wake me up!'

She gave such a yell when she opened her eyes and found him there. He sat back on his heels laughing like a drain, and as he did, something on the field caught his eye.

The field was so full of colour and movement that the woman stood out a mile – tall and slim in a plain grey dress, walking unhurriedly towards them across the grass. He saw her from a long way off. He thought maybe she was from the school office with a message for one of them, because she was walking straight as an arrow towards them, past everyone else, not even turning her head to look.

If she was from the office, they'd find out soon enough. He lay down in the grass again, closed his eyes and said the rhyme. As he opened them there was a scream and everyone fell about laughing, because they'd done Ginny again. He sat up and as he did, he looked back across the field. The woman in the grey dress had stopped now. She was still a way off but was just standing there, looking at them.

There was time for one more game before the bell. Everyone lay back down and closed their eyes, and as Richard closed his, he felt a shadow settle over his face, and felt the cold of it. A strand of hair brushed against his cheek. There was someone with their face over his. He knew it was Ginny, she had the longest hair.

'One, two, she's coming for you,
Three, four, knocks at the door,
Dead Molly poison my cup,'

What did that bit mean anyway? he thought.
'Dead Molly wake me up!'

He snapped his eyes open ready to push Ginny away—
only it wasn't Ginny.

Pressed right up against his face, was a face he didn't know at all – a woman's face, dead and white, her skin bloodless and transparent, her eyes black as coal.

'Jesus!'

He sat bolt upright in his bed, his breath stuffed in his chest, his heart hammering. The playing field, the summer's day had gone and he could see his room all around him; his hands on the bedclothes, his wardrobe, the half-open bedroom door, the landing light on. He could hear the sound of his mum in the kitchen downstairs. He swept his hair back, his heart slowing, his breath coming more evenly. He'd never, ever had a dream like that before. God, it had been so real.

He could still picture the woman's face inches away from his, the clear blue sky behind her.

But it was dark outside – it wasn't even summer. For the moment, he was so thrown by the dream that he wasn't quite sure what time of year it really was.

'Come on, Richard! You'll be late for school!'

He got out of bed, put his feet in his cold slippers and his dressing gown on.

It had snowed in the night. He parted the gap in the curtains and looked down at the street – at the sodium orange lamps and the sodium orange snow piled thickly on the rooves and bonnets of the parked cars.

In the bathroom, he looked at his face in the mirror and tried to forget the dream, but it felt like it was only inches away from him still. He turned on the tap and the water ran for a moment, then dribbled to a stop. He turned it off and on again, then the cold one too, but no water came out of either.

'We've got no water!' he shouted.

'You'll be late,' answered his mum.

'But there's no water!'

She didn't answer him.

He went back into his room and got dressed in the cold, standing against the radiator.

When he got downstairs and sat in the kitchen, he knew at once there was something wrong. His mum looked at him like she did when she was angry – like she did when there was something simmering that hadn't been put right – but he couldn't think what he'd done that it might be. Without a word she put the cereal bowl down on the table in front of him, and the cereal box next to it, then she stood with her back to him watching the pan of milk on the cooker.

He'd been going to tell her about the dream – about how real it had all been – but that didn't seem important any more.

'What's up, Mum?' he said.

She didn't answer him.

He heard the milk hiss and rise in the pan. She turned the gas down, and poured the hot milk into his bowl. Then she looked straight at him.

'You know, I've never loved you,' she said.

He grinned at her, but she didn't smile back, and the grin died on his face.

'Not like I love your brother,' she said. 'I really love him. But you? You're not even second best.'

He sat there with his mouth open. He kept expecting her to say the thing that would turn it all into a big joke. But she didn't.

'I didn't even want you,' she said. 'You were just a mistake. You're not even your dad's boy.'

He stared at her. He felt physically sick. He could feel everything that he believed in, everything that he loved, crumbling to dust around him.

'Why are you saying this, Mum?' he whispered.

She pursed her lips and shrugged.

''Bout time you knew it,' she said.

She dropped the milk pan into the sink and turned the tap on, but no water came out. The tap just made a thumping noise like someone knocking at a door, louder and more insistent, until he realised that there really was someone knocking at the back door.

Thump. Thump. Thump.

His mum didn't even bother to look up.

'You'd better open it,' she said. 'It's about all you're good for.'

Wordlessly, he stood up and reached out for the handle. The knocking was getting more demanding.

Thump! Thump! Thump!

He turned the handle and as the door opened he felt the cold damp chill of the snow outside, and out of the dark stepped the tall pale woman in the grey dress, her face dead and white, her skin bloodless and transparent, her eyes black as coal.

He sat bolt upright in his bed, his breath stopped in his chest, his heart hammering, and all around him was daylight – bright summer daylight in his own room.

His heart was racing, he could see the bedclothes, the room, the sunlight streaming in through the window. There was birdsong and the radio from downstairs.

His mum stuck her head round the bedroom door.

'Did you call?'

'No,' he said unsteadily. 'Just a bad dream. Oh, Mum – that was the worst. I thought I was awake but it was still a dream.'

'Well, get yourself up,' she said. 'Blow the cob-webs away.'

He got out of bed, and went into the bathroom – looked at his face in the mirror, then turned on the tap at the sink. The water ran for a moment, and dribbled to a stop. He stared at the empty bowl. He turned the tap off and on again, then he tried the other – but nothing came out.

He felt the skin on the back of his hands crawling cold.

It was just like in the dream.

He hesitated.

'We've got no water,' he called, slowly.

'No. They're doing work at the end of the road,' answered his mum. 'I meant to tell you. It's been turned off. I've got water in a pan if you want to wash.'

She brought the pan up the stairs.

When he got down into the kitchen and sat at the table, she put a cereal bowl in front of him, and the cereal box next to it, then she stood with her back to him watching the coffee pot on the cooker.

It was like the dream, only not the dream.

He glanced uneasily at the back door, but there was no knock.

'Our Frank's coming home this weekend,' his mum said brightly.

He was Richard's older brother, just gone to uni in the autumn.

'It will be lovely having him back,' she said, her face all lit up. 'Not half the same when he's not here, is it?'

The coffee gurgled in the pot and she poured Richard a mug. He looked at her face as she did it – saw how pleased she was that Frank was coming home – and he realised that she never smiled at him the way she smiled at Frank, and that made him feel awful – all small and cold inside. Like he'd felt in the dream.

'You love me too, though, don't you, Mum?'

'Course I do,' she said.

But she didn't look at him as she said it, she turned away, and it seemed to him that she was only saying it because she had to, not because she really meant it.

He ate his breakfast in silence, but he looked up at her and he just couldn't shake that thought off. That she didn't really love him at all.

Maybe he was just a mistake? Was it something he'd never been meant to know?

He didn't remember getting to school, he just found himself there, walking through the gate with all his friends. He was trying to tell them about the dream – how he'd been on the field, and then at home, and how that had been a dream as well, and that he'd woken up from one dream and found himself in the other – and he wanted so much to try and say something about his mum, but he didn't even know how to start – and they'd just laughed, because it all sounded so dumb when he said it, only it hadn't been.

'It was so real,' he said.

But they just laughed more.

It was a hard sort of laughter, like stones against a roof. It didn't sound like they were laughing because what he was saying was funny, it sounded like they were laughing because he was the joke – as though he wasn't their friend at all, just someone who hung around them.

'Don't laugh at me,' he said.

Only that made them laugh more, and the laughter felt like poison.

Ginny put her arm round him. She glanced knowingly at the others as she did it, like the fact that he fancied her was a joke they were sharing, and over her shoulder he caught a glimpse of a scrap of grey – of someone coming towards him through the crowd of white shirts and blouses, only there were so many blouses and so many shirts that he couldn't see who it was. He looked at Ginny, and she smiled.

'It's all right,' she said. 'You've just got to understand.'

'Understand what?' he answered.

She put her hand to his face and kissed him full on the lips. Her mouth was cold and wet, and her breath smelled like stale meat. He tried to pull away, but she held her hand against the back of his head and kissed him again.

'You've just got to understand,' she whispered. 'I've come to wake you up.'

And it wasn't Ginny any more.

It was the thin woman in the grey dress and her face was bloodless, and dead and white, and her eyes were black as coal.

His eyes snapped open and he found himself out of his bed, stumbling on the cold floor of his bedroom before he even knew where he was. He stood there, shaking, a sheen of cold sweat on his skin as the room took shape around him. It was morning.

The sun was streaming through the window, the radio was on downstairs. He could hear his mum singing.

Glass-eyed he went down the stairs.

His mum was pulling washing out of the machine. She looked up.

'Hello, honey,' she said. 'You need a shirt?'

He just stared at her.

'Is this real or a dream?' he said.

Whatever she'd been going to say, she changed her mind and frowned instead.

'Are you all right, love?'

When he didn't answer, she put the washing down and stepped towards him, but he backed away, bumping clumsily into the wall.

She looked at him with concern in her face, and then smiled.

'You're not really awake yet, are you, love?' she said gently.

His eyes widened.

'So this is a dream?'

She put her hand out and touched him. He could feel the weight of it – the lovely warmth of it – against his skin.

It felt like a real hand.

'Come on,' she said, and she shook him by the shoulder. 'You wake up, now.'

He stared at her.

'You love Frank more than me, don't you?' he said.

She shook her head and smiled again.

'Come on, don't be silly. You need to wake up. You've got to get to school. Get yourself upstairs, get yourself dressed, and get yourself out.'

He looked past her at the table. There was no bowl, no box of cereal. No pan on the cooker. Not like in the dream.

He turned and went slowly back up the stairs, still not sure.

In the bathroom he turned on the tap, and the water dribbled to nothing.

There was a card propped behind it, with his dad's writing – 'no water' it said. Then in capitals, 'WASHER!!!'.

His mum called up the stairs.

'You can't use the hot tap.'

He picked up the card and held it between his fingers. It was damp and he could see where the biro had smudged. He ran the cold tap, and water came out of it.

But was it real?

He washed, dressed and got himself out to the bus stop. He stood in the warm morning sun looking at the trees and the houses, at the passing cars and people's faces. The colours were so vivid, so real. He found himself staring at the woman next to him in the queue, not sure if he'd ever seen her at the stop before.

Waiting for her face to change.

'Excuse me?' she said.

'I'm sorry,' he said, and looked away.

The journey passed like silk around him. He felt so tired. He pinched the back of his hand until he broke the skin – he could feel the hurt of his nails, but still he wasn't sure if any moment now he was going to wake up. When he came to his stop he left his bag on the seat. He was halfway down the bus before the woman behind him called him back and lifted up the bag for him. His eyes widened and he caught his breath, but she was just a woman on her way to work, holding up his bag.

'Don't forget this,' she said.

When he got to school his friends were standing on the path at the edge of the field, their bags on the ground around them. He looked at their faces as they talked, and it felt like he was watching a film of them standing there, talking.

'Is this a dream?' he said.

No one paid him any attention.

'Is this a dream?' he said, louder, catching hold of one of them, Karl, by the front of his shirt. The shirt tore in his hand and the button came off, but he didn't let go.

'Is this a dream!'

Karl shoved him away – saw that his shirt was torn and pushed him again, angrily, and then they were actually fighting. It started just like that. The others pulled them apart, and Richard put his hand to his lip and it was bleeding. Karl was staring at him red-faced.

'What's got into you, dude?'

'I'm sorry,' he said. 'I'm sorry.'

They signed in at tutor and everyone knew that Karl and he had had a fight, but they were all trying to pretend it hadn't happened, only it had. He could feel his lip, fat and sore – like he'd got his finger on it and was pushing it against his teeth – and there was a big rip in the front of Karl's shirt.

When they'd done tutor, some of the others were talking about walking down to Tesco and buying stuff to make up a picnic, but he didn't want to go and they stopped asking him. They just left him be.

He thought he had things to do in the library, but he couldn't remember what they were, so he sat at one of the tables by the bookshelves. As he sat there someone came up behind him and put their hands over his eyes, and he thought it was the woman and he pulled the hands away, knocking his chair over as he leaped up – but it was Frank.

It really was Frank. He was back for the weekend.

He looked different – he'd bought new clothes at uni, new shoes, and his hair was short – but it was Frank all right. He'd already rung their mum to let her know he was here and she was coming in for lunch – she hadn't known he was coming either, it was a big surprise for her too. He said they could all go and have coffee together.

As Frank and he walked into town their mum passed them in the car, stopped and picked them up. She got out of the car and gave Frank such a hug. Richard sat in the back and listened to the two of them talking in the front. His mum was so happy to see Frank. They didn't even seem to notice him. He watched their faces as they turned and chatted – they were so easy together, her and Frank.

And he knew she loved Frank more.

The realisation came like some dark little flower blooming in his head – Frank who'd got into uni, Frank who everyone liked more than they liked him, Frank who could play football, Frank who could never do anything wrong.

For the first time ever, he hated him. Wished he hadn't come home.

The car started making a knocking sound from

underneath. His mum and Frank looked at each other, startled by it, and then they started laughing as the knocking got louder and louder.

They just kept laughing, it wasn't even funny – they just kept laughing.

His mum was still laughing as she turned around to look at him, only it wasn't his mum – it was the thin woman, dead and white, and she wasn't laughing any more.

He opened his eyes with a start—

he was lying in his bed.

There was no car, no Mum, no Frank. Only his bedroom and bright morning.

He began to cry.

He cried huge, hopeless tears that slid down his face and fell onto the sheets. He screwed the sheets between his fists and pressed them to his eyes.

The house was silent.

Propped against the bottom of his open door was the toy blackboard they wrote messages on. In green chalk were the words, 'Taken car to garage. See you after school'.

His mum had drawn a little car and a smiley face underneath it.

He sat on the edge of the bed until he had no more tears to cry.

In the bathroom, he looked at himself in the

mirror. His face was empty and there were dark half-moons beneath his eyes. He turned the tap on, and the water dribbled to nothing in the sink.

Like a dead man he walked past the bus stop, through the people in their bright summer clothes, the mothers with prams and toddlers, through the traffic and the green trees.

At school he didn't even bother to talk and no one seemed to notice. He was waiting for it to happen. Waiting for the thin woman to come.

But she didn't.

At lunch he found himself lying on his back with the others in the long grass at the edge of the field. Next year someone would have passed their test and have a car, but not yet.

It was such a hot day. The sky so blue, so clear – boys with their sleeves rolled up, girls barefoot, carrying their shoes on the tips of their fingers.

Ginny sat up.

'Let's play Dead Molly,' she said.

'No!' He shook his head. 'I'm not going to play that.'

But he was the only one who didn't want to play – it was such a good game. They used to play it all the time. He watched them as they lay down and closed their eyes, saw Ginny creep up and quietly put her face over Karl.

'One, two, she's coming for you—'
'No!' said Richard.
But they didn't stop.
He looked out across the field, his eyes searching for the tall woman in the grey dress, but he couldn't see her.

'Three, four, knocks at the door,
Dead Molly, poison my cup,
Dead Molly, wake me up!'

Ginny screamed, Karl yelled and everyone laughed—
and that was all that happened.
No thin woman, no dead face against his, just the sound of voices on the playing field and the bell ringing for the end of break.
They picked up their bags and trailed in from the field. He kept waiting for it to happen, but it just didn't, and in a way he couldn't explain – in a way that felt like relief, like the passing of something dark and wrong – everything was suddenly more real.
It was like lightness.
He couldn't really remember what had happened in the evening, but the end of the day came and he climbed into bed and slept, dreamlessly.

But he might just as well have closed his eyes and opened them again, because suddenly it was morning. There was a frost on the road outside the window. The trees were bare, and he knew that was how it should be.

In the bathroom the taps worked, the water steamed into the sink, and he put the plug in and watched it fill. He looked at himself in the mirror, and it was him. It really was him and he felt such a wave of relief.

This was the real world.

It was daylight, and it was real.

He could hear the radio on downstairs.

He got dressed by the radiator and went down, sat at the table and his mum asked him what he wanted.

And he said, 'Toast.' And she didn't know why he laughed when he said it.

She cut the bread and put it under the grill, and as she did her phone buzzed on the side.

'You keep an eye on these,' she said, and she picked up the phone and opened a message. He saw her face brighten.

Something cold began to creep through him.

She was looking at the phone, reading the message, and her face had a wistful look to it.

'It's not the same when he's not here, is it?' she said.

Richard stared at her. It felt as though the world was sliding from beneath him, he felt the skin on the back of his hands crawl cold.

There was a knock at the back door.

'That'll be Pam,' his mum said. 'I said I'd give her a lift. I'll do the toast, you do the door. Go on.'

The knocking came again, louder, more insistent.

He put his hand on the door and hesitated.

His mum was already turning the toast.

The knocking came louder still.

His mum turned and looked at him over her shoulder.

'Go on, then,' she whispered, then silently mouthed the words.

'Open it.'

Now even the pool of light the lantern cast was getting smaller and smaller, drawing the boy closer to the man.

'I don't want to hear any more stories,' the boy said.

'You should have told me one of your own then,' said the man. 'Can't say I didn't give you a chance, can you? Can't blame me for doing all the chin-wagging if you're not going to do any.'

'I don't know any stories.'

'Don't know the capital of Egypt, don't know any stories – what's the world coming to?' He laughed. 'Come on – Jack and Jill, there's one. Hickory Dickory, there's another.'

'They're nursery rhymes.'

'Still stories.'

'For babies.'

'Still stories,' the man said. 'That's what I'm wanting to hear, you see. I'm wanting to hear your story. Everyone who gets off the train gets the chance to play my little game. I ask them for a story, and if I don't like it they get to play my little game.'

It was as though that thing that had been creeping out of the dark had arrived. The boy hadn't believed it would, but now it was here.

'I'm not going to play,' he said

'You don't know what it is.'

'I'm not going to play it!'

The man didn't answer.

He turned and looked at his bag. It sat on the bench next to him – cheap brown leatherette, frayed at the handle, with dead leaves and dead flowers – all dry and shrivelled – poking out of the top.

'I expect you're wondering about my bag,' he said, patting it and looking back at the boy. 'Toby and me have been collecting flowers. Nothing like a nice bunch of flowers to brighten a place up.'

'They're dead,' the boy said.

The man looked at the flowers.

'No,' he said. 'Bit of water, that's all they need. Little bit of water in a pot. Have them right as rain.'

'Is this the game?' the boy said.

The man looked up at him and smiled. A thin smile.

183

'You've got to tell me a story first,' he said.

'All right then,' the boy said sharply. 'Here's a story: stupid old man keeps telling a boy who got on the wrong train – and is cold and tired and fed up – stupid stories he doesn't want to hear. The end. There, that do you?'

The man looked at him carefully. For several moments he didn't say anything, then he said, 'And?'

It wasn't what the boy had expected.

'And what?' the boy answered.

'And what happened then?' the man asked softly. 'What was the end of the story?'

The boy couldn't think of anything more.

'Then the train came,' he said uncertainly, 'and the boy got on it and went home.'

The man pursed his lips as though thinking about this very carefully. The little dog sniffed at the boy's foot. The man looked down at it and tugged at the lead, as though it was a distraction to his thoughts.

'Oh no,' he said at last. 'That won't do. That won't do at all.'

'What do you mean?' said the boy.

The man smiled.

'For a story,' he said. 'It won't do for a story. Where's the bit that happens in between? The bit between me telling the stories, and you getting on the train. Where's that bit gone?'

184

'There isn't another bit,' the boy said.

'Oh, but there is,' said the man. 'I didn't like your story, so there's my little game.'

The boy took a step back, but behind him was dark, deep as a void.

'I'm not going to play it,' he said.

'Which one did you like the best?'

'I didn't like any of them.'

'No . . .' the man said shaking his head. 'You have to say which one you liked the best.'

'Is this the game?' the boy said.

The man beamed.

'This is the bit I like the best,' he said. 'Go on, tell me which one.'

The boy shook his head almost in disbelief.

'You mean, I've just got to say one?'

'That's it. Train will come,' said the man. 'Always comes after we've played my little game. I tell you what I'll do – one last story to help you make up your mind.'

The Black Forest Chair

'It was a complete steal,' his mum said. 'It was under all this stuff right at the back of the shop – I'm not sure they even knew they had it.'

She was always poking around in junk shops, and everything she brought home was always 'a bargain', always 'a complete steal' – always a pile of rubbish. Their house was full of the stuff already – 1950s lampshades, Formica tables, cupboards with sliding glass fronts. It was hard to find room for anything else, but somehow she always seemed to manage it.

'Come on,' she said. 'Help me get it in out of the car.'

Jos put down what he was doing and followed.

Whatever it was, it was wrapped in a blanket – and that was all he could see. She'd had to put the back seat down to get it into the boot, and as he tried to pull it out the blanket came loose, but his mum covered it up again so he couldn't see what it was.

'Not till we get in,' she said.

It was made from dark wood, he'd glimpsed that much at least, and it felt like a chair, but the blanket was all the wrong shape for that – not enough bits sticking out – and it weighed a tonne.

'You get this in on your own?' he said.

'No,' she said. 'Man at the shop helped me.'

With effort they carried it through the door and stood it in the middle of the little front room. It only just fitted. His mum stood there grinning, her hand on the top of the blanket.

'Tah dah!' she said, and whisked it off like some showman in a theatre.

Jos stared.

'You're kidding me!' he said. 'That is so cool.'

Beneath the blanket was a black oak chair. No wonder he hadn't been able to make out what shape it was – the front of it was a wooden seat with legs carved like the trunks of small trees, the arm rests were like that too – curved branches with oak leaves winding through them. But the back of the chair was the thing.

It was a solid carved bear.

There were no back legs to the chair, the bear just stood upright holding the arms and the seat in two huge paws. Its mouth was open to show its teeth. At some time they'd been painted but the paint was made to look old and tobacco stained, like the wood of the chair.

'Go on, sit in it,' his mum said.

Jos settled himself into the seat and leaned back against the bear's head. The muzzle was hard and knobbly and just about head height. It wasn't comfortable at all.

'Was it some kind of advert?' he said.

'No,' she said. 'It's really old – from Germany. I

saw one like it in a magazine once. I knew what it was soon as I saw it.'

He craned his head round and looked at the bear again with new attention – at the black wooden muzzle and the black carved eyes. It looked like it might have been old, but then his mum bought any old tat.

'What did you pay for it?'

'Nowhere near what it's worth,' she said.

'Is it worth a lot?' he asked, suddenly more interested.

'Might be,' she answered. 'But I don't think I'd want to sell him.'

She never wanted to sell anything. When his mum bought something, it stayed bought. He only had to look around the house to see that. She tilted her head to one side as though admiring the bear's better features, then picking up Jos's beanie from the back of the sofa, she popped it over its head.

'Look,' she said. 'He's smiling.'

Jos looked at the bear, and it seemed to him that if it was smiling, it wasn't that friendly a smile – the eyes were too hard and there were far too many teeth for that.

In fact he wasn't quite sure what he thought about the chair at all, and that didn't change over the coming week. It was all right during the day time, but in the half-light at the end of the day he'd stand and look at it, and there was something that he didn't like. Something uncanny-valley about that bear, as though if Jos were to turn away and then quickly back, he might just catch it move. His mum only laughed at him when he told her that, and all his friends thought the chair was a complete joke – they'd take it in turns to sit on it when they came round – but they didn't have to be there at the end of the day as it grew dark, not like Jos did.

It was maybe the week after his mum had brought it home that the clocks went back. He came in from school to an empty house, threw his bag down, made himself a cup of tea and sat on his own in the front room, looking out along the darkening street while he flicked through the messages on his phone. It was one of the days when his mum worked, so she wouldn't be in for an hour yet, and though it wasn't dark enough to put the lights on, shadows had begun collecting in corners and, unusually for him, he felt uncomfortable being on his own in the house.

He found he'd sat in the black wooden chair. He wouldn't normally have chosen it, and it was almost a surprise to him that he had, but it had been a long day and he couldn't be bothered to move. So he just sat there with his mug of tea and his phone, looking out at the street. There was something soporific about the smoothness of the wood under his hand, and he could feel the hard muzzle of the bear on the back of his head. It felt damp, as though his own breathing was really the breathing of the bear against his neck.

The change, when it came, was so sudden that there wasn't even a pause between the two moments – maybe he'd looked down at his phone and then up – but he wasn't in the front room any more. Same chair, same clothes, but not the same place. His phone just showed a screen of white noise.

He closed his eyes and opened them again, but nothing changed. He was sitting in a small, low kitchen with a stone floor under his feet and dark wooden beams above his head. The beams were wound with dried flowers and leaves, and between them hung bright copper pans and cooking knives and ladles. A fire was spitting and crackling in an iron stove as though a bundle of sticks had only just been stuffed into it, though there was no sign of anyone who might have done that.

He sat open-mouthed, staring about him, because dreams didn't begin like this. It felt more like some complicated trick and he half expected his mum or someone else to come in and laugh, and tell him how it had been done.

Only they didn't.

The fire crackled and spat. He could feel the warmth of it against his face.

At one end of the room was a small window, and at the other a black oak door. Between them, the plaster was covered with paintings, all bright and garish. He looked at them more carefully. In one a woodsman, half-wolf, half-man, was howling at a moon that shone through the branches of the trees. He carried an axe in one hand and a head by its hair in the other. Beside him was a picture of two children – lost and starving – walking across a carpet of leaves through a wood that was full of eyes. The third was a little man with a sharp, bright knife. He was crouched at the bottom of a sleeping child's bed, his hand drawing the covers away. Jos sat unwillingly looking at that one for several moments. It was so full of threat. Then his eyes moved on to the next. A carter lay on a lonely muddy track through a forest, with his head crushed beneath the wheels of his wagon, and in the last, a coffin gaped open and empty in a churchyard at night.

They were disturbing in a way he couldn't even begin to describe – as though each one was a picture of something that had actually happened.

He sat staring at them. He might have sat there longer still, but the longer he sat the more anxious he felt. Somewhere, someone had to be watching him, laughing at his confusion. He knew that if he were just to get up and look around, he'd find out soon enough how all of this was being done. So he stood up and peered through the glass of the window. A deep fall of snow carpeted the ground outside, and a path disappeared between thick fir trees into a deep, dark forest.

However the trick had been done, the world outside the window looked perfect. Even the glass felt cold to touch. He breathed on it and wrote his name in the condensation. Then he noticed the ticking of a clock and he looked about to see where it was.

The clock was in a case on the wall. The case was the size of a small cupboard, though the face was smaller than a saucer and painted with delicate little flowers. Weights hung beneath it, and a pendulum swung slowly to-and-fro behind them. The whole thing was carved to look like a forest with a cottage hidden, all secret and deep amongst its trees. He looked again at the window, at the snow and trees outside, then again at the clock. This was the same cottage as on the clock, the same forest outside the window.

From inside the case a whirring began and, as he watched, the front of the cottage popped open. One by one a scene of little painted wooden figures began to move slowly, in fits and starts, through the rooms of the house. They were the same as the figures painted on the walls. When the mechanism finally lurched to a halt it was only the little man with the bright knife that was left. It was a relief when the front of the cottage snapped shut and he couldn't see the little man any more.

He glanced then, uneasily, at the other things in the room. He didn't know how this trick had been done, or why, but he wanted it to stop now. He crossed the stone floor and laid his hand on the iron latch of the black oak door, lifted it and pushed.

It took a moment for his eyes to adjust to the darkness that was there, and for him to realise where he was.

He was standing in the open door of his own wardrobe.

He could see his bed and the shadowed shapes of things on the floor, all outlined against the light of the street lamp behind his curtains. Behind him through the wardrobe door he could see the little kitchen, the case of the clock and the paintings on the wall, but no light came from that place into his bedroom, not even from the snow-bright window. His room was velvet dark, and silent.

By the single crack of light that came through a gap in the curtains, he could see himself lying in the bed, see his own face on the pillow – eyes closed in sleep. The bed was arranged just like the bed in the picture painted on the plaster wall, right down to the sheets turned back, just so. All that was missing was the little man with the bright, sharp knife in his hand, and suddenly Jos knew whose cottage in the woods it was.

He just knew.

He glanced back at the day-lit room and, reaching out to his own bed, he shook his sleeping self by the shoulder, because he knew he had to wake up – but the sleeping him wouldn't wake. It didn't so much as stir, no matter how hard he shook it. He could feel the warmth of his own sleeping body like it was another person's, and that was so strange a thing, because it was him.

With that certainty of dreams, because that is what he told himself this must be, he knew he had to leave himself some sign, something that on waking would prove to him that all this had happened, and then he would know that the wardrobe door was going to open in the night while he slept and let in a little man with a razor sharp knife.

He pulled a handful of dried flowers and leaves from one of the beams in the bright kitchen and, shutting the wardrobe door behind him, he strewed them in the dark over the bottom of his bed like a meadow of warning. Then he stopped and listened.

For a while he heard nothing, then distant and far away – as if from over a hill and through a forest and a fall of deep snow, he heard a rasping sound – like a knife being sharpened on a stone.

The light in his face was so sudden, so bright, he had to shield his eyes with his hand.

'What you doing sitting in the dark?' said his mum.

She'd banged the door open with the bags of shopping and flicked on the light switch with her chin.

'I thought you were out it was so quiet.'

His phone had slipped from his fingers to the floor, and he leaped from the chair as though it had bitten him.

His mum pulled the curtains closed – asking what had happened in his day, and what he wanted for tea – but he hardly heard her.

It had been so believable – was still believable, even on waking.

He went through the house turning all the lights on – the landing, the bathroom, his bedroom – then stood looking uneasily at his wardrobe door and the covers of the bed, and it felt as though he'd only been there a moment ago and seen himself asleep. He half expected to see the dried flowers strewn there, but there were none. Not even sure it was safe to do, he opened the wardrobe door, but there was nothing there either, only junk and clothes, and the back of it was just white plastic and wood.

He felt so stupid. Relieved and stupid.

But when he came to go to sleep that night it didn't seem so stupid at all. It seemed so very real again – as though the only thing in the whole room was the wardrobe door. He didn't want to turn the light out. He sat with his bedside lamp on and his back against the headboard, watching the door. He heard his mum turn off the lights downstairs and come up to bed, heard the heating switch off and the radiators cooling down, but he still didn't want to turn the lamp out. Its light seemed thin and cold and the dark on the landing even darker as the night dragged past, but he didn't want to turn it off. He tried leaving the wardrobe door open so that he could see what was inside, but somehow that only made things worse – as though something might actually part the clothes as he watched – and he got out of bed into the cold and shut the door again. Put his sports bag against it so that he could hear if it opened.

But finally, it was only sleep that crept into his room and took him.

Jos opened his eyes not having thought he'd even closed them, and found the world full of daylight.

The first thing he did was to look at the bottom of his bed, smooth his hand across the crumpled covers, but there were no flowers, no leaves – nothing but bright daylight, and it rubbed all his night fears away.

The days that followed served to do the same thing, and though he couldn't help looking uneasily at the wardrobe before he turned his light out at night, by the end of the week he was never as convinced as he had been that first time that it held any terrors other than those he might imagine. It was just a wardrobe. The same was true for the dark oak chair. For those first few days afterwards, he'd pass it like he might a dog that had recently bitten him, but by the end of the week it was just a wooden chair, and the bear was just a wooden bear, and the teeth were just wooden teeth.

He even sat in it.

As the days passed, the nights drew in – he needed to put the lights on as soon as he came home from school, and it was quite dark by the time his mum got in. It was a surprise then when coming home one evening he opened the door of the house to find the big oak chair stuffed into the darkness of the little hall in front of him. It hadn't been there when he'd left for school in the morning and the only thing he could think of was that his mum had wanted to move it and had got it this far before she went to work. It was too heavy for her to manage it on her own, but even so, she could have left it somewhere else.

He had to stand on it and clamber across to reach the light switch.

He shut the front door behind him, stood on the seat and stretching for the light, he felt the world tip and suddenly the darkness about him wasn't the darkness of the hall but of somewhere else. The streetlight that had shone through the window above the front door was now moonlight across the stone flags of a floor.

He knew where he was at once, only this time he wasn't alone.

Someone was lighting the oil lamps that hung from the ceiling between the ladles and pans. There wasn't enough light for Jos to see who it was, all he could see was the spill of burning wood in the person's hand. They were reaching up and lighting the lamps one by one. The wicks guttered and flared, and out of the darkness slowly emerged the paintings on the wall, all garish and shadowed, and, reaching up to light the lamps, a little man with a face creased like an old apple whose teeth were stained and filed to points sharp as needles.

Jos didn't dare to move.

Even with the lamps lit, there wasn't enough light to drive the darkness from that room, but there was quite enough for the man to see Jos by, only he didn't so much as look at him. He lit the lamps, shook the spill of wood into the fire and, reaching up to one of the beams, took down a long, steel knife. Jos watched him do it. He watched as the man sat himself at the table and, laying the blade across his lap, began to sharpen it with a small stone. In the flickering light of the fire, the edge of the blade glittered like a razor.

Only once did the man pause. Turning he looked over his shoulder, straight at Jos, but it wasn't Jos he was looking at. He was looking at the carved clock on the wall, as though he was waiting for the clock to strike.

And strike it did.

With a whirring of cogs the front popped open and the little figures moved again in fits and starts through the rooms – the woodsman with the axe, the little man with the knife.

The man watched them. He pushed back his chair and, crossing to the clock, tapped the dial with his nail as though to satisfy himself upon some small point of time. And then he looked at Jos. He looked right at him and grinned, and it was a wicked grin – sharp toothed, dark and full of malice.

Jos floundered from the chair as something that

smelled of rubber was pushed against his face and there was light so bright that it hurt—

and voices and faces

and his name being spoken

and he was on the floor in the hall and there were men in green overalls bending over him.

'You fell off it,' his mum said.

'I was trying to reach the light switch,' he said for the hundredth time.

'You didn't have to stand on it, you fool. You were out cold when I got in. I couldn't wake you up. I didn't know what to do, that's why I called them. You gave me such a fright.'

They'd done the whole business – wrapped in a blanket in the back of an ambulance to casualty, the wait in the little curtained cubicle. He'd got a lump the size of a goose egg on his forehead, but he could count how many fingers the doctor held up and follow them too, and that had been enough for the hospital. Now they were home again, hours later, in the kitchen with a mug of tea and a box of parac- etamol. His mum had wrapped a packet of frozen peas in a towel and he was holding it against his head.

'I just wanted to clean behind it,' his mum said.

'You didn't have to leave it in the hall.'

203

'You didn't have to stand on it.'

They'd been through it already, he couldn't be bothered to argue any more. Besides, his head hurt so much.

He took himself upstairs, washed his face and brushed his teeth then looked at the lump – all hard and black and purple – in the bathroom mirror. He felt too sick and too tired to even care about a little man in the wardrobe as he got into bed. There are some things that are so real they make nonsense of pretend fears, and cracking his head on the bottom of the stairs was one of them. There was no little man with a knife going to come out of his wardrobe. Dreams like that were just what you got when you smashed your head against the stairs.

All he wanted to do now was to sleep.

He put his head on the pillow and closed his eyes, he didn't even dream, it was as though he just fell into dark, soft, silence.

But something woke him. Some noise.

He opened his eyes and lay listening in the dark of his room, not sure what it had been. His mum must have gone to bed because there were no lights on and the house was quiet and still. All he could hear was the click of the radiators, they sounded like the ticking of a clock, only it wasn't them that had woken him.

He lay and listened.

Through the crack in the curtains, light from the street outside fell across his pillow. In the shadowed dark he could see the shape of the wardrobe against the wall, and the outline of his things on the floor.

He closed his eyes, but he knew that something had woken him. Something he could not put a name to. He sat up and looked again at the dark of the room. Then he reached over and turned on his light.

At the bottom of the bed, the covers were strewn with a handful of dried flowers and leaves.

The man reached down and scratched the little dog on the top of its head. 'Getting late now, isn't it, Toby?'

He looked up at the boy and for all that his face framed a smile, it didn't touch those shard-glass eyes. They glittered in the light of the lantern.

'Which one did you like the best?' he said.

'You mean, I've just got to say one.'

'That's it. You get to choose.'

The boy stood with his mouth open. He could almost have laughed, only it didn't feel like a joke. He didn't know what the man meant – did he mean he had to choose the one that had frightened him most, or the one he wanted to hear again? He didn't want to hear any of them again. Or maybe the man had a book of them in his pocket and he was going to give him one to take home.

Only, they didn't feel like book stories.

The man sat, looking intently at him.

'Swallow a fly like that,' he said.

The boy closed his mouth.

He could feel the stories moving, like dark ink in darker water – the candle, the light, the car, those children, the photos, the soot boy, the dead woman, the chair – he could hear them like whispers – and he didn't want to have to say any of them.

The man leaned forward.

'Train won't come until you do,' he said quietly.

The boy shook his head – if that's all the man wanted, he'd say one and be done with it.

'All right,' he said suddenly, and said the first one that came into his head. 'The one with the car.'

The man looked steadily at him.

'You can change your mind,' he said.

But the boy didn't say anything.

The man held up a finger in the air, as though he was going to say something more, but he didn't. He was waiting for the boy to hear what he'd heard—

a hissing in the rails.

The boy turned round and looked back along the dark platform. Slowly, round a distant curve, a light was coming – a long snake of light.

'The train!'

He ran down the dark platform towards it waving his arms, terrified it wasn't going to see him. It had slowed for the halt and he could see the driver in his cab as he passed. He turned and ran next to the cab, could almost keep up with the window, but it was slowly pulling away from him. He banged the flat of his hand against the glass and saw the driver turn in surprise and look at him, the driver's face wide in amazement. Then the carriages slid past the boy, all lit up. He could see men inside in their big fluorescent jackets. Then he heard the brakes of the train squeal as it ground to a halt and stopped.

The driver got out of his cab. A man opened one of the doors and put his head out to see what was happening.

'What the bloody hell do you think you're doing?' shouted the driver.

'You going back to Parkside?' the boy answered. 'I got on the wrong train. I got off here. I've got to tell my dad where I am.'

He was almost in tears. He just wanted to be on the train, off the platform.

An older man in a big yellow jacket stepped down from a carriage.

'You all right, lad?' he said.

'I've got to tell my dad.'

208

The carriage had tables filled with plastic cups of tea and bowls of sugar, bottles of milk. The men were looking at him – tired men with working faces, hard-lit in the carriage strip lights.

The man in the yellow jacket gave him his phone, and the boy climbed into the warm carriage and the doors closed behind him.

In the light spilling from the windows he saw the concrete wall along the platform begin to slide past. Saw the bench and the lamp poles – and for a moment he saw in the darkness the old man, standing with his lantern and his bag and his dog, and the man was looking right at him – only, it wasn't dead leaves and dead flowers that were sticking up out of his bag any more. It was a big toy car, all silver chrome and red paint. The boy glimpsed it only for a moment, then the platform fell away and there was just the long line of carriage windows, black like mirrors, with reflections of the men and the tables, and the cups and bottles of milk, all strip-lit bright.

The train got to the station at Parkside before his dad did, home was a fifty-minute drive away. There were a couple of station staff about, but apart from them the place was deserted. The coffee concession in the hut on the platform was all shut up and locked. But at least it was a real station, not some cold slab of concrete in the middle of nowhere.

He sat outside the closed ticket office, wrapped his coat round him and waited – watching the minutes tick past on the big station clock. But if he closed his eyes he could hear the man's voice again – see that dark platform against the inside of his lids – so he got up and walked about instead, and even then when he turned round he half expected to see the man with his lantern and his dog coming along the platform towards him.

When his dad finally got there the boy wanted to tell him what had happened, but the first words his dad said were, 'You'd better have a good reason for this one, son', and the way he said it sealed up everything inside the boy. He tried to tell him about the stories and the game, but it was as though his dad didn't hear. The only part his dad heard was that he'd got on the wrong train and that there'd been an old man walking his dog, and that wasn't what the boy had wanted to tell him at all. And he didn't get to say anything else, because his dad told him how stupid he'd been, and asked whether he thought he'd like to drive halfway across the country in the middle of the night just because someone couldn't be bothered to get on the right train, and he said it so sharply

210

*that there wasn't an answer, and they got in the car
and drove home in silence.*

*His mum was still up when they got in, but it was
the small hours and the house felt strange-shaped
and empty. She sat with him at the big kitchen table,
and he tried to tell her what had happened, but he
was too tired. He could barely put one word next to
another by then, and finally he realised that his mum
and dad weren't angry, they were just happy to sit
there with a cup of tea because he was safe, and
that's all that mattered to them.*

*As he climbed the stairs, his dad called after him.
'Who's stupid, then?'*

*But his dad had a smile on his face as he said it.
'Got a surprise for you,' his dad said.
The boy frowned.
'Go on, you get to bed. I'll show it you in the
morning.'*

*He undressed like a dumb thing, all the familiar,
homely things of his room around him. He fell into
bed and pulled the duvet over his head. But as he
closed his eyes he could see the old man again – tapping his feet, popping a mint into his mouth.*

'Nice bit of fish.'

*And he couldn't get those stories out of his head.
They filled the darkness of his room, chasing him
round and down into a dreamless sleep.*

By the time he woke, half the day had gone. The winter sunlight was bright across his room. When he went downstairs he knew at once there was a secret in the house that his mum and dad weren't telling. He could see it in their sideways looks. His little brother almost gave whatever it was away, and their dad had to hold up a finger to him and go 'whoa, whoa, whoa!' before he let it slip.

'If you'd got home on time yesterday, you'd have seen it then,' his dad said. 'But you have to get on trains that go to the right places to do that.'

They took him outside, made a big thing of it, only there was nothing there to see, just the garden. It was such a bright day, and so far from the night before that the boy wasn't sure any more if that had even happened. His dad made him close his eyes, made him promise not to open them till he was ready. Then he steered him by his shoulders across the grass and down the path to the garage, and then he stopped.

The boy stood for a long moment with his eyes shut waiting. He heard his little brother laugh and his mum shush him.

He heard his dad lift up the garage door.

'You can open your eyes now,' his mum said.

They were standing there, the three of them,

212

smiling like there was no tomorrow, and inside the garage behind them—

inside the garage behind them was a big American car, all bright red paint and shining chrome—

'Rock and roll!' said his dad.

Acknowledgements

I would like to thank Linda Sargent and Andy Barnett for their never failing friendship and support, the calm and resourceful Jenny Savill who deserves golden medals for calmness and resourcefulness, Bella Pearson and Hannah Featherstone for editing and copy-editing, Dave Shelton for cover and illustration, and the whole team at DFB who took my story and made it into the book you are holding in your hand.